Chocolate

"Careful," Andrea sa[...] contest inside the w[...] million-dollar wrappe[...]

Bess read the instruc[...] wrapper. " 'Play the Crown Jewels contest and win. Look inside to see if you're a winner.' " She rolled her eyes. "I already know the answer: 'Sorry. Try again next time.' "

"Just remember who bought these candy bars for you if you strike it rich." Andrea pointed a finger at Bess. "I'm sure you're planning to donate half the proceeds to the Science Sleuths, right?"

Bess laughed as she unwrapped her candy bar. "Of course. Absolutely. Unfortunately, we both know that half of nothing is noth—" She gasped as she looked down at the wrapper in her hand.

"What is it?" Nancy asked.

Bess showed her the words printed on the inside of the wrapper in gold letters.

Nancy's blue eyes grew wide. " 'Congratulations,' " she read aloud. " 'You've won the grand prize.' "

Nancy Drew
Mystery Stories

Available from MINSTREL Books

NANCY DREW® 151

THE CHOCOLATE-COVERED CONTEST

CAROLYN KEENE

A MINSTREL® BOOK

Published by POCKET BOOKS
New York   London   Toronto   Sydney   Tokyo   Singapore

A MINSTREL PAPERBACK *Original*
A Minstrel Book published by

POCKET BOOKS, a division of Simon & Schuster Inc.
1230 Avenue of the Americas, New York, NY 10020

Copyright © 1999 by Simon & Schuster Inc.

ISBN: 0-671-03443-X

First Minstrel Books printing September 1999

10 9 8 7 6 5 4 3 2 1

NANCY DREW, NANCY DREW MYSTERY STORIES, A MINSTREL BOOK and colophon are registered trademarks of Simon & Schuster Inc.

Cover art by Ernie Norcia

Printed in the U.S.A.

Contents

THE
CHOCOLATE-COVERED
CONTEST

1

Golden Bar

Bess Marvin squeezed her eyes shut and screamed. Her face was white. Her long, blond hair flew out behind her.

"Ow," said her friend Nancy Drew as Bess's fingers clamped around her arm.

Eleven-year-old Laura Marquez patted Bess on the back. "Don't be scared, Bess. It's only the kiddie coaster."

George Fayne turned and grinned at her cousin, Bess. "Hey—I thought *we* were supposed to be the chaperons here."

Bess grunted as the brakes screeched and the ride jerked to a halt. "I'll be chaperoning on the ground from now on, thank you very much." She hopped out of the car and took a moment to steady herself. Then she held her arms above her head. "Okay, Science Sleuths! Over here!"

The children gathered a few feet from the exit, and Nancy counted heads. "Ten, plus three chaperons. Excellent. We're all accounted for."

So far so good, Nancy thought as she pushed her reddish blond hair from her eyes and looked down at the sea of people moving through Kings Commons Amusement Park. It wouldn't be hard to lose a sixth-grader in this crowd. The Science Sleuths were antsy from their three-hour bus ride that morning from River Heights and needed to move around.

"Find your buddy," Nancy instructed the group. "Make sure to all stay together."

She led the Sleuths across a drawbridge painted with fire-breathing dragons. Street musicians wearing kilts played an old Scottish tune. Below them, rafts bobbed in a river of churning rapids.

"Can we go on the Moat Float later?" Emma Lim asked.

"Sure." George glanced up at the darkening sky. "Assuming it doesn't rain."

Kenny Fox groaned. "It rains every single time I go to an amusement park."

"We're coming back tomorrow," Nancy reminded him, "and the forecast is for sun."

"Two days enveloped in the aroma of luscious

chocolate." Bess closed her eyes and inhaled deeply. "Boy, am I hungry."

Kenny took a chocolate bar out of his pocket. "Want some?"

Bess looked at the candy. She laughed. "Kenny, that's a Golden Bar."

"So?"

"So, we're surrounded by several tons of chocolate made right here at Royal Chocolates headquarters." She gestured toward the enormous factory on the other side of the parking lot. "Yet you brought your own chocolate all the way from River Heights."

Kenny shrugged. "I like Golden Bars better." He popped a square of chocolate into his mouth as they passed under a rose-covered trellis that led into an English garden.

"There's Andrea." Nancy waved at a petite woman with brown hair sitting on a bench ringed by mums.

Andrea hurried over to meet them. "Hello, everyone. Are we enjoying Kings Commons?"

"This is the best field trip ever," Laura said. "I bet nobody else ever went to an amusement park to *learn* stuff."

"Actually," George said, "when Andrea was our high school physics teacher, she brought our class here, too. Of course, we called her Miss Cassella then."

"And I got sick on Miss Cassella's new shoes after riding on Labyrinth," Bess said. "Which may be the reason she gave up teaching to start the Science Sleuths."

Andrea laughed. "Not at all. It was because of inquisitive students like you that I realized the need for a science enrichment program in our community. And it's handy to have former pupils lecture on things like how detectives use science to solve crimes. As our real-life sleuth Nancy Drew will do. It can also be handy for former pupils to chaperon. Actually, I might have asked someone else if I'd remembered what you did to my shoes, Bess." Andrea winked at her.

"When are *we* going to get to ride on Labyrinth?" Laura asked.

"I heard it's faster than Royal Pain," Kenny said.

"We have to wait till we ride them both before we pick which coaster's faster," Noah said. "Then we'll do the calculations to test our hypothesis." He tossed his pencil into the air. "I can't wait."

"You might have to wait." George squinted at the purple aluminum tracks in the distance. "Is that a car stuck there on the loop?"

Nancy checked with a Kings Commons employee. "Royal Pain is temporarily out of service," she told the disappointed Sleuths. "They're not sure when it will be fixed."

"But we can ride it before we leave, right?" Tyler asked.

"If it's fixed," Andrea said.

"And if it's not fixed, we'll come back next year and ride it ten times," Tyler said. "Right, Andrea?"

Andrea forced a smile. "We'll see."

"Hey." Bess put an arm around Andrea's shoulders. "You seem upset. What's wrong?"

Andrea spoke softly so that the Sleuths wouldn't hear. "I don't want the kids to know, but I can't promise we'll come back to Kings Commons next year. I can't even promise the Science Sleuths will be in business next year."

"Oh, Andrea, I'm sorry," Nancy said.

Andrea tore a leaf from a bush trimmed into the shape of a crown. "I always knew it would be tough running a nonprofit corporation. These kids' parents pay what they can, but most of them can't afford much, and there's no way I'm going to raise the tuition. I'm months behind in payments for our lab equipment. If I can't afford to do experiments the way I want or bring in speakers or take field trips, this program is worthless." She sighed. "I've been looking for a corporate sponsor, but so far I haven't had any luck. I'm afraid my funds are just about exhausted."

"Wait," Bess said. "What about those relatives of yours with all the money? I know you were nervous about asking them since you haven't spoken in so many years, but don't you think it's at least worth a try?"

Andrea shook her head. "I *have* tried. Several times. But they won't take my calls. They were my last hope." She watched the Sleuths swapping yo-yo tricks in the shade of a chestnut tree. "I'm really going to miss these guys, though."

She walked over to the Sleuths. "Are you ready to get going?" she asked them.

"Andrea, I'm hot," Noah said.

"I think it's going to rain," Kenny said.

"I'm hungry," Emma said.

"I think it's time for a surprise," Andrea told Bess. "However tight our resources might be, a trip to Kings Commons would not be complete without these." She pulled out a box of chocolate bars. "Who wants a Crown Jewels bar?" she asked the Sleuths. Ten hands shot into the air.

"I thought so."

"Kenny," Bess said, "didn't you just eat a candy bar?"

"Yeah," Kenny replied, "but I've got room for another one."

"Excuse me," called a high-pitched voice from behind Nancy.

"Oh. I'm sorry." Nancy scooted over to make way for a chubby, red-cheeked blond woman who was pushing her way through the crowd. The woman had a candy bar clenched in one hand, her husband's elbow in the other. They appeared to Nancy to be in their early thirties.

"I can't believe Royal Pain is broken again," the woman complained. "Come on, Phil. We have to— Oof!" She reeled backward as she crashed into Kenny.

"Pardon me," Kenny said.

"Please tell me those grubby fingers did not touch me." The woman looked down and inspected her white shirt. "I knew it. Why don't you look where you're going, young man? This was a very expensive shirt, and if these chocolate stains don't come out—"

Nancy cleared her throat. "Ma'am, I'm sorry about what happened to your shirt, but it wasn't Kenny's fault."

"You walked right into him," George said.

The woman's face turned redder. "This whole vacation is turning into a royal pain, isn't it, Phil?" And she marched away, dragging her husband.

"What was her problem?" Kenny asked Bess.

"I don't know. I don't understand how anybody can be so grumpy while eating a chocolate bar."

Andrea held out the box of chocolates. "Would the chaperons each like a chocolate bar?"

George held up her hand. "Thanks, but I'm trying to avoid junk food."

"I'll have one." Nancy took it from Andrea and

tucked it into her purse. "I think I'll save it for a rainy day."

"That might be today." Bess chose a chocolate bar and tore open the wrapper.

"Careful," Andrea said. "There's an instant win contest inside the wrapper. You wouldn't want to rip a million-dollar wrapper, would you?"

Bess read the instructions printed on the outside of the wrapper: " 'Play the Crown Jewels contest and win. Look inside to see if you're a winner.' " She rolled her eyes. "I already know the answer: 'Sorry. Try again next time.' And with the amount of chocolate I eat, you know I will."

"Just remember who bought these candy bars if you strike it rich." Andrea pointed a finger at Bess. "I'm sure you're planning to donate half the proceeds to the Sleuths, right?"

Bess laughed as she unwrapped her candy bar. "Of course. Absolutely. Unfortunately, we both know that half of nothing is noth—" She gasped as she looked down at the wrapper in her hands.

"What is it?" Nancy asked.

Bess showed her the words printed on the inside of the wrapper in gold letters.

Nancy's blue eyes grew wide. " 'Congratulations,' " she read aloud. " 'You've won the grand prize.' "

8

2

Secrets and Spies

"No way," George said. "Nobody really wins those contests, do they?"

"Not *nobody,* but pretty close." Nancy squinted at the fine print on the wrapper. " 'Number of grand prizes awarded: One,' " she read. " 'Odds of winning the grand prize: approximately one in four million four hundred thousand.' "

Noah's mouth dropped open. "Wow."

"If you're not going to eat your candy, Bess, could I have it?" Kenny took the chocolate from Bess's limp hand. "Thanks."

Tyler elbowed his way to Bess's side. "Let me see."

"No, I want to see," Emma said.

Bess swallowed hard. "Just a second." She held the wrapper over their heads. "I'll read it to you: 'The grand prize includes one million dollars in cash, one trip for four to Kings Commons Amusement Park in Royal, Illinois, and thirty Crown Jewels bars per month for twelve months. Employees of Royal Chocolates or Kings Commons and their immediate families are not eligible to win. To claim your prize, make a photocopy of the winning wrapper. Mail the original to—' "

"That building right over there," George finished for her, pointing to Royal Chocolates headquarters.

Noah was scribbling numbers in his notebook. "Do you realize, Bess, that if there are ten thousand people at Kings Commons today—and I bet there are judging by the length of these lines—you'd have to fill up about four hundred amusement parks this size to find four million people? So to be the lucky *one* out of four million is pretty astronomical."

"I'll say." Bess blinked. "It doesn't seem real."

"It'll seem real when you've talked to the people at contest headquarters," Nancy said. "So why don't you walk across the parking lot and do that right now."

"And could you ask them," Katie piped up, "about the trip to Kings Commons? Like, do they think you could substitute another prize?"

10

"Or maybe you could give the trip to someone else," Emma suggested.

Bess laughed. "I don't suppose you have someone else in mind?"

"Enough!" Andrea said. "Let's give Bess a break and let her talk to the contest people. She'll bring us news in a little while. In the meantime let's go on one more ride and then have lunch—on Bess."

Bess smiled weakly. "Thanks. But do you think you could spare Nancy? I'd really like some moral support."

"We've got everything under control," George assured her. "Take your time."

"We'll take a ride on High Tea." Andrea pointed to the oversize rose-patterned teacups that crossed overhead, carrying passengers from one side of the park to the other. "We'll have lunch at Uncommonly Good and meet you at the Moat Float at, say, two o'clock."

"That sounds great. We'll see you then." Nancy felt a drop of rain on her face. She pulled her hair back from her face and wound it into a ponytail.

"Thanks for coming with me, Nan," Bess said as they waited to have their hands stamped at the exit gate so they could reenter. "Holding on to this wrapper makes me very nervous."

Nancy grinned. "You've checked your pocket about five times in the last two minutes."

"I know. It's weird to think that one little piece

of paper can be worth so much money. If Andrea hadn't said something to make me look, who knows? I might have thrown it in the trash." Bess took a deep breath. "Anyhow, I'm glad I'll be able to help the Sleuths stay in business."

Nancy smiled. It was just like her friend to think of others first. "Bess, you know Andrea was joking. She wouldn't hold you to your promise to give half the money to the Science Sleuths."

"I know," Bess said, "but I want to help—and now I can."

Nancy squeezed Bess's hand. "You're such a good person, Bess Marvin."

"I'm a very lucky person." Bess looked up at the six-story brick administration building and read the sign above the main entrance: "Welcome to Royal Chocolates. We treat you Royally." She brushed a drop of rain from her eye. "I'll say."

Bess and Nancy approached the receptionist's desk. "That's the biggest candy dish I've ever seen," Bess whispered.

The receptionist smiled. "Help yourself."

"Thanks." Bess took a crown-shaped chocolate wrapped in purple foil.

"Hi," Nancy said. "We were hoping you could help us. My friend just won a prize in the Crown Jewels contest. And since we happened to be in the park, we were hoping we might be able to come and claim it in person."

12

"I'm sorry," the receptionist said. "The marketing department is too busy to handle the small prizes. They're dispensed from another location. So if you would just mail a copy of the wrapper—"

"But it's not a small prize," Bess interrupted. "It's the grand prize."

The receptionist sat up straighter. "The grand prize?"

Bess nodded.

"Okay," she said slowly. "Why don't you have a seat? Someone from marketing will be with you in a moment."

"She seemed surprised when I said I won the grand prize, didn't she?" Bess commented as they watched the receptionist make a phone call.

"I guess it's pretty unusual for people to walk in off the street and claim their prizes," Nancy said.

"Yeah. I wonder what the odds are of getting the winning wrapper while you're actually in the park. One in a hundred million?"

The receptionist motioned for them to approach the desk.

"They're expecting you upstairs in marketing," she said. "That's on the fifth floor. Take a right when you get off the elevator and wait in the reception area. Joyce Palmer is the contest administrator. She'll meet you there shortly."

Nancy pressed the Up button beside the elevator. "Thanks for your help."

On the fifth floor the chocolate brown walls were hung with prints of Royal Chocolates wrappers through the decades. Warm chocolate-chip cookies were spread on a table beside a carafe filled with cocoa. "If I worked here, I'd gain fifty pounds," Bess whispered. She poured herself a cup of steaming hot chocolate and took a sip. "Ow!" she cried.

"Burned your tongue?"

"With something this good, there's always a price," Bess murmured.

Nancy took a cookie and closed her eyes as she savored the taste of butter and chocolate mingling on her tongue. She was startled out of her reverie by the sound of an irate male voice.

"Joyce!" the man shouted.

"Joyce," Nancy whispered to Bess. "She's the person we're supposed to see, right? Maybe she's coming to get us."

Bess tapped her foot. "I hope so."

"Joyce!" the voice repeated. "In my office. Now!"

"Then again, maybe she's not." Nancy relaxed in her seat and popped the rest of the cookie into her mouth. "I'm going to have to get the recipe for these," she murmured.

"Yes, Mr. Tumey?" said Joyce in a high-pitched voice.

"Tell me, Joyce. Why is it that our company holds contests?"

14

Nancy felt her muscles tense and glanced over at Bess. Although they could not see what was going on in Mr. Tumey's office it was clear from his tone that he was very upset. Nancy was afraid they were about to overhear an unpleasant conversation.

"I'm not sure what you're asking," Joyce stammered. "I mean, you know why we—"

"Why do we run contests?" Mr. Tumey repeated.

"We run contests," Joyce replied, "to entice shoppers to buy our candy with the prospect of winning a prize. It gives us an edge over the competition and increases our sales."

"Not only have we not increased sales," Mr. Tumey shouted, "but they have dropped by ten percent. We have made an outlay of millions of dollars in prizes and marketing materials only to *lose* money!"

"I can't stand this." Bess cleared her throat loudly.

Mr. Tumey's voice continued to get louder. "Can you understand why this makes me upset? Why this makes *my* bosses upset?"

"Of course." Joyce's voice wavered. "It makes me upset, too. But no one could have predicted this would happen."

"That's your job, Joyce. You have to be able to predict this kind of problem."

"But you were enthusiastic about the contest—you and Mr. Castle approved the idea."

"We approved the idea based on the facts that you presented to us," Mr. Tumey said. "It was your responsibility to do the research."

Nancy squirmed in her chair. She wondered whether Mr. Tumey would be yelling at Joyce if he knew there were visitors in the office.

"That Mr. Tumey sounds mean," Bess whispered. "I'm glad we don't have to talk to him."

"I presented you with all the facts we had at the time," Joyce said. "Obviously I couldn't have predicted that Pleasant Candies would launch a new candy at the exact same time that we ran our promotion. I couldn't know that Golden Bars would be a caramel-filled candy bar just like Crown Jewels."

"They do taste the same," Bess whispered to Nancy.

"It was your job to know," Mr. Tumey said. "Market research is your area. Furthermore, do you think it's a coincidence that Pleasant Candies launched this new candy bar at the same time we ran our promotion? That they undercut our price by five cents? That they duplicated the taste of the Crown Jewels chocolate? Somebody at Pleasant knew our plans, Joyce. Pleasant Candies is paying someone to steal our secrets."

Joyce gasped. "Are you saying you think there's a corporate spy?"

"I know there's a corporate spy." Mr. Tumey paused. "I want you to stay alert, Joyce. We have to find this person before Pleasant carves out a greater share of our business. Before something else happens. Do you understand?"

"Yes, Mr. Tumey. I'll do what I can."

"See that you do."

Nancy stood as Joyce strode out of the office with her head down.

"I'm sorry," Joyce said. "Can I help you?" Then her hand went to her mouth. "Oh, no. I'm Joyce Palmer. You're waiting to see me, aren't you? I completely forgot."

"Yes," Nancy said apologetically. Joyce must know that they had overheard Mr. Tumey's every harsh word, she thought.

"We're sorry to bother you. We know you must be busy." Nancy shook Joyce's hand, then introduced herself and Bess.

"The receptionist said something about your wanting to claim a contest prize. I don't know why she sent you to me." Joyce bit her lip. "But come have a seat in my office. We'll see if we can take care of it for you."

Joyce offered Nancy and Bess some hot chocolate.

"No, thanks," Bess said immediately, her tongue going to the roof of her mouth.

Joyce settled into her chair. "All right, then. What can I do for you?"

"This is kind of hard to believe, but"—Bess fumbled around in her pocket for the wrapper—"I seem to have won the grand prize in the Crown Jewels Sweepstakes."

There was a long pause. "The *grand* prize?" Joyce repeated.

"Yes. You know, a million dollars, a trip to Kings Commons . . ."

"I'm sorry," Joyce interrupted. "But what you're saying is absolutely impossible."

The smile froze on Bess's face. "I'm sorry," she stammered. "I don't understand. Why is it impossible that I won?"

"Well," Joyce said, "there's only one grand prize. And it's already been awarded."

3

Jungle Kingdom

Nancy and Bess stared at Joyce.

"What did you say?" Bess asked.

"You probably misread the wrapper." Joyce took a swig of coffee. "It happens all the time." She motioned for Bess to hand it to her. "Let me see. I bet you won one of the smaller prizes. A Crown Jewels tote bag or something."

Bess unfolded the wrapper and showed it to Joyce. "It clearly says 'grand prize,' " Bess said. "One million dollars."

Joyce frowned as she flattened the wrapper on her desk. She pulled a magnifying glass from her desk drawer.

Bess leaned forward. "I'm not wrong, am I?"

19

"You're not wrong," Joyce confirmed. "But— the winning wrapper has already been verified by our contest prize division. In fact, the winner is enjoying her vacation at the park right now. And there's only one winning wrapper. Only one was printed." Joyce paused for a moment to let her words sink in. "Do you understand, then, why I find your claim disturbing?"

"I'm sure you understand why we find your claim disturbing," Nancy said. "Are you saying that Bess has cheated in some way?"

"Nancy is a detective, and her father's a lawyer," Bess blurted out. "They'll prove that I won fair and square."

Joyce put her hand over Bess's. "You don't need a detective or a lawyer, Bess. Of course we'll do a thorough investigation of your claim. Let me make a copy of the wrapper for you to keep. The original will be sent to the claim investigators."

Bess picked up her wrapper and clung tightly to it.

"It's standard procedure for all prize winners," Joyce explained.

Nancy nodded to Bess, and Bess handed over the wrapper.

Joyce moved to a locked file cabinet and removed a folder from the top drawer. "How old are you, Bess?"

"Eighteen," Bess replied. "Why?"

"Excellent," Joyce said. "Contest rules state that you must be at least eighteen to win. I'll need you to sign these affidavits to that effect. You must also verify that you are not directly related to an employee of Royal Chocolates or Kings Commons, and that you are not employed here yourself."

Bess took the pen from Joyce. "I have no problem with any of that. Where do I sign?"

Nancy glanced over Bess's shoulder. "Do you mind if I read these first?"

"Of course not." Bess handed her the papers. "Thanks."

"In the meantime, let me ask you a few questions," Joyce said. She ran her fingers through her brown curls. "Where did you purchase the winning Crown Jewels bar?"

"I'm not exactly sure," Bess explained.

Joyce raised her eyebrows.

"What I mean is, I'm at Kings Commons with a nonprofit educational group called the Science Sleuths. Their leader, Andrea Cassella, bought us the chocolate this morning from one of the vendors in the park. I'm not sure which one."

Joyce set down her pen. "That's very interesting."

"Why is that interesting?" Bess asked. "It's no big deal. I'm sure I can find out where she bought them."

"I'd like you to find out," Joyce said, "because we're not selling the instant-win bars inside the park."

Bess opened her mouth, then closed it again. "Look," she said finally, "I don't know what's going on here, but I didn't cheat. I wouldn't cheat, and if you want to accuse me of cheating, you're going to have to prove it."

"I'm not accusing you of anything," Joyce said pleasantly. "As I explained, we'll look into the matter."

"You can bet Nancy will be looking into the matter, too." Bess stood up. "Come on, Nan. Let's go."

"Don't forget to sign your paperwork," Joyce said.

Nancy gave Bess the papers. "Everything looks okay to me. Do you want me to ask my dad to review them?"

"That's okay. I just want to get out of here." Bess seized the pen and scrawled her signature in several places.

"Make sure you list your address and phone number so we'll be able to contact you," Joyce said.

Bess nodded. "And I can be reached at the King's Quarters Motel tonight."

Joyce opened the supply closet, which was filled with Crown Jewels hats and canvas bags and

T-shirts. She stuffed several chocolate bars into a bag and gave them to Bess. "For your students," she said. "I hope you enjoy your stay at Kings Commons." She smiled. "Do you have big plans for your day?"

"Well," Bess said, "since the Royal Pain is broken and it's raining and Nancy and I wasted half our day here, I guess that leaves the animal park."

"Oh, you'll enjoy Jungle Kingdom." Joyce rifled through her desk drawer for a brochure. "You'll want to be sure to see the baby white tiger." She stood and shook each of the girls' hands. "I apologize for the inconvenience and any offense you might have taken. I promise I'll be in touch as soon as I have news."

"Thanks," Nancy said. "We'll see ourselves out."

As they walked into the reception area, a woman barreled into Joyce's office, brushing against Nancy's sleeve.

"Does that woman ever watch where she's going?" Bess mumbled.

Nancy realized it was the same woman who had run into Kenny earlier in the park. Her husband followed a few paces behind her.

"Hi, Diana. Phil," Joyce greeted the couple cheerfully. "What can I do for you?"

"I was wondering whether a new shirt might be included in my all-expenses-paid trip," Diana said. "Mine was soiled by a careless kid in the park. I got a huge bruise on my knee, too."

"All-expenses-paid trip?" Bess pressed her hand against her mouth. "Do you mean to tell me that nasty lady is the real contest winner?"

"Not the *real* contest winner," Nancy corrected. *"You're* the real contest winner."

"Right. And how much do you want to bet that next she'll try suing them over her stupid bruise." Bess shook her head as they moved to the elevator. "I'm so glad you're here, Nan. I know you'll be able to figure out what's going on."

Nancy put a hand on Bess's shoulder. "Don't worry. I'll do everything I can to prove you're the real winner." She stared back at Joyce's office. "And I think I'll start with a close look at Diana and Phil."

The weather had turned dreary, and a steady rain fell on Kings Commons. Nancy saw Bess shiver and suggested that they stop and buy parkas before meeting the Science Sleuths at the Moat Float. They ducked into a country store with a candy cane–striped awning.

George waved at them from behind a display of sweatshirts. "Hey, guys. We came in here to get out of the rain. How'd it go?"

Ten Science Sleuths rushed to Bess's side.

"What happened?"

"Where's the chocolate?"

"I won't be getting the money until later." Bess patted the tote bag. "I do have chocolate bars— for later," she added firmly.

Bess then picked up a book and absently flipped through pages of dessert recipes. After a minute George nudged her. "What's up? You're looking at chocolate and you seem totally unexcited."

"I'll tell you later," Bess murmured. "How was the Moat Float?" she asked the Sleuths.

"We got really wet," Laura said with relish. "But you can hardly tell now that it's raining so hard."

"I knew it was going to rain." Kenny sighed. "Our whole day's ruined."

"Not ruined." Andrea clapped her hands. "Come on, Sleuths. We're going to take in the Jungle Kingdom from our van, where it's dry and cozy. Find your partners. Let's go."

As the group trudged across the parking lot in the steady rain, Nancy quietly filled George and Andrea in on their meeting with Joyce.

George frowned. "What a way to do business. You can bet I won't be buying Royal Chocolates anymore."

"George, you never bought Royal Chocolates," Bess said.

"Okay, well, *you* shouldn't buy them anymore, then," George suggested. "That'll really hurt their business."

Bess punched her cousin's arm. "Very funny."

"I think I can clear up one mystery here." Andrea unlocked the van and motioned for the Sleuths to climb in. "If Joyce says your claim is suspicious because Royal isn't selling instant-win bars in the park, you can tell her I didn't buy them in the park."

"You didn't?" Nancy examined a Crown Jewels bar from the tote bag Joyce had given Bess. She noticed that, as Joyce said, the wrapper did not advertise the instant-win contest.

"You know we're pinching pennies," Andrea explained. "Crown Jewels bars were on sale at a grocery store last week in River Heights, so I bought them then."

"You plan ahead for everything, don't you?" Bess said with admiration.

"Obviously not," Andrea replied. "Otherwise, I would have made sure you knew where I got the candy before Joyce grilled you about it. I'm sorry about the confusion."

Bess waved her hand. "That's okay. You can bet we'll be talking to Joyce again soon."

Andrea gave Nancy some papers to hand out to the Sleuths as Bess made sure everyone's seat belt was fastened.

"A scavenger hunt. Cool!" Laura exclaimed as Andrea turned the key in the ignition.

Noah read the first item on the list. "In this relationship, the female rules the roost. I think," Noah said, "that the correct answer is a member of the bird family. Not that we'll be seeing any today. Even birds have sense enough to stay out of the rain."

Nancy peered out the window. The animal park appeared deserted, although it was difficult to see more than a few feet in the gray gloom.

"This is no fun," Tyler complained.

"Hey!" Emma shouted. "Someone's throwing candy at me."

"Come on, guys," George coaxed. "Let's settle down."

Andrea turned up the windshield wipers a notch. "Maybe we should go back to the motel and wait out this storm."

Nancy opened her mouth to agree, but she was cut off by Bess's scream.

A car sped around the curve moving toward them, and Andrea had to turn the wheel sharply to avoid hitting it. Nancy caught a glimpse of the midsize white sedan speeding away before Andrea lost control and the van veered off the road and down a slippery slope. There was a jolt as they hit a wire fence and stopped suddenly.

For a moment there was silence.

"Is everyone all right?" Nancy asked. She heard Laura sniffling. "Laura. Are you hurt?"

Laura shook her head. "N-n-no. Just scared."

"Don't shake your head," Nancy said gently. "Just answer yes or no. Does anyone hurt anywhere?"

There was a weak chorus of nos.

"I'll bet that was more exciting than Royal Pain," Kenny said.

The Sleuths laughed, and the tension was broken.

Once they were certain no one had been hurt, Nancy peeked out the window to see where the van had come to rest. The front tires were sunk in a muddy stream of water.

Andrea groaned. "I'm so sorry."

"It's not your fault," Bess assured her. "That car came out of nowhere."

"The accident was definitely the other driver's fault," Nancy said. "I didn't get the license plate number or even the model of the car because it was going so fast."

Noah tapped Andrea's shoulder. "Um, do we have to walk all the way back to the motel?"

"The van might be okay to drive," George said.

"Why don't we get out and take a look?" Nancy suggested.

She and George climbed out of the van and moved carefully on the muddy hillside.

Nancy ran her fingers over the yellow lettering on the side of the van. Science Sleths, she read. A tree had scraped off the U entirely.

"This doesn't look too promising." Nancy bent to examine the front tires. "We're sunk three inches in this mud."

"Uh, Nan . . ." George stood slowly. "Do alligators eat people?"

"Please tell me there isn't a reason you're asking that right now," Nancy said, following George's gaze. Half-submerged in the water near their feet was a seven-foot reptile, its muscles tensed as it slid out of the stream.

4

A Day at the Park

"George," Nancy cried. "Get inside the van!"

She heard shouts from inside the van and realized the Sleuths had spotted the reptile, too. It lifted its head in response to the noise and rose completely out of the water, its short legs churning.

Nancy sprinted to the other side of the van. Before she got there, Bess had the sliding door open. Andrea reached out and helped pull Nancy and George inside.

Nancy collapsed into her seat as Bess slammed the door shut. "Go away," Bess shouted to the retreating reptile.

Nancy saw that Bess's face was white. "And to

think we were complaining a minute ago that all the animals were hiding," Bess said.

George plopped down across from Nancy. "I guess alligators don't mind the rain."

"That wasn't an alligator, George." Noah pressed his nose against the window. "It had a long snout, and its lower teeth were visible when it closed its mouth. That means it was actually a crocodile."

Nancy shuddered. "It was close enough for you to see its teeth?"

Noah nodded. "Oh, yes."

"Did you know that a crocodile often drowns its victim before eating it?" Ashley asked.

"No. I didn't know that." Bess locked the door to the van. "And I definitely don't think we'll be going back out there."

"We're trapped," Emma said. "Like sardines in a can."

"Unlike sardines in a can," Bess pointed out, "we're alive."

"But how are we going to get out?" Emma rolled down her window. "Help!" she shouted.

"Shh," Andrea said. "We've disturbed the wildlife enough for one day. There's no need to panic."

"Even if it were safe to go outside, we'd never be able to push the van out of the mud," Nancy told Andrea. "We need a tow truck."

Andrea pulled a cell phone from the glove compartment. "And we'll get one. Sit tight, everybody."

While Andrea made the call, Laura pulled out a pack of Kings Commons playing cards. "I bought these in the Candy Shoppe. Does anybody want to play?"

Bess surveyed her hand a few minutes later with disgust. "Do Kings Commons cards have extra kings? I think they all went to Noah."

Nancy set her cards down as she heard a vehicle pull up behind them. "That must be the tow truck."

"Whoa," said a man's voice. "This is not exactly what I pictured when you said van. This here is more like a minibus."

"Be careful!" Andrea called out the window. "There's a crocodile out there. We just had a close call."

A man and a woman wearing khaki Jungle Kingdom uniforms hopped out of the tow truck. "You don't need to tell us, ma'am," said the man. "Not that there would be any danger from Crocus if our nice, expensive fence were intact." He kicked at the sagging wire where the van had broken through.

"Crocus?" Bess asked.

"The crocodile," the woman explained, peering into the murky water. "You've scared her indoors.

The keeper radioed that she's closed in her pen. That means it's safe to move around out here."

"Great," George said. "Let's get out of this van."

The chaperons helped the kids down. "Watch your step," Bess repeated to each of them. "Watch your step in this mud."

Andrea ran a hand over the side of the van. "Look at this dent."

"That'll cost a couple hundred dollars to fix," the tow truck driver said.

"Do you think we can drive it?" Andrea asked him.

The driver shook his head. "No, ma'am. The wheel rim's bent. It'll be in the shop at least a day."

"At least a day?" Andrea turned to Nancy and her friends. "But we're supposed to go home tomorrow evening."

"Sorry," the driver said.

He went to work attaching the tow truck to the van under George's watchful eye as Nancy, Bess, and Andrea climbed the hill with the Sleuths. Meanwhile, Hal and his partner began patching the damaged fence.

"The Sleuths' parents are *not* going to be happy," Andrea mumbled. "I'm not looking forward to telling them I need to keep their kids for an extra day. And how am I going to pay for another night in a motel—not to mention the van repairs?"

"Look," Bess said, "I just won a million dollars—I think. Now, I know I won't get the money right away, but half of it is yours the minute I do."

Andrea shook her head. "You really don't have to do that."

Bess smiled. "I know I don't have to, but I want to. Anyhow, given the shabby way the contest people have treated us—I mean, they practically accused me of cheating—I think the least they owe us is a free night at the motel."

"I agree," Andrea said, "but I doubt they'll be so gracious. In fact, I'm sure they won't." She took Bess's hand. "I appreciate your offer, Bess, and we can discuss it later when things are settled. For now, the motel fees will go on my already over-taxed credit card."

"I wish there was something we could do for you now," Nancy said.

Andrea grimaced. "I don't suppose you'd care to help me call ten sets of angry parents regarding our extended stay at Kings Commons?"

"That's a tame assignment," Nancy assured her. "You can count on us."

After a trip back to the motel to change into clean clothes, the Sleuths returned to the park for dinner.

A mock jousting session went on below them as they feasted on roast chicken and vegetables.

"Are we really eating like kings?" Tyler asked Andrea.

"I don't think kings used plastic knives and forks," Andrea said.

Bess set down her plastic fork with a contented sigh. "I don't care. I was starving."

George nodded toward a woman at an adjacent table who was eating a double hot fudge sundae. "I think that woman could eat anyone under the table."

Bess narrowed her eyes. "I'd like to leave her there."

"That's Diana, owner of the alleged winning wrapper," Nancy murmured to George.

"Ah," George said. "I recognize her now."

Diana and Phil were looking at large black-and-white photographs of themselves taken at the park. "Queen Diana and King Phillip. The last time I'll wear a tiara, I'm sure," Diana said. "Do you think we should reprint our company brochures with these photos? Diana and Phil Nugent, president and vice-president . . ." She stopped when she spotted Nancy watching her.

"You know what, Phil?" Diana said. "I think I just lost my appetite." She crumpled her napkin and stood.

"Don't leave on our account," Andrea said. "You haven't finished your dessert."

"Why don't you just help yourselves?" Diana snapped.

"I don't think so," Andrea said sweetly. "I'm allergic to nuts. Not to mention rudeness."

"You tell her, Andrea," Kenny said. "She tells us all the time how she's allergic to rudeness," he explained to Diana.

"Well, I think *I'm* allergic to children," Diana told Kenny. "If you'll excuse us." She scraped her chair along the floor as she pushed it up to the table. She and Phil stalked out of the restaurant, leaving her sundae melting.

"I wonder why Diana is so rude to us?" Nancy asked Bess that evening in their motel room. "She seemed quite pleasant when she was talking to her husband tonight."

"Until she saw us," Bess said.

Nancy nodded. "Exactly."

Bess slipped off her tennis shoes and massaged her feet. "She said she hates kids. She probably finds the Sleuths a little overwhelming." She fell back on the bed. "I love them, but they *are* tiring."

George hung up the phone. "Okay, I talked to Emma's parents. After we call Kenny's, we're done." She waved the receiver at Nancy and Bess. "Any volunteers?"

Bess groaned and rolled over on her stomach.

Nancy laughed. "I'll do it. I want to call my dad when we're through, anyhow."

When Nancy reached her father, she told him about her meeting with Bess in Joyce's office. Carson Drew was a criminal defense attorney, but Nancy felt sure he would know something about the legal implications of Bess's situation.

"Well," Mr. Drew said when Nancy had finished, "that's some story. I presume you're on the case?"

Nancy laughed. "Yeah, I guess I am. But I wanted to see if there was anything else we should be doing. Legally, I mean."

"You know this isn't my area of expertise," Mr. Drew said, "but it sounds to me as though you've done fine so far. Let me know if you have any specific questions, and I'll ask an expert."

Nancy thanked her father. "You're the best. And please send Hannah my love. Oh—tell her I bought her a great cookbook. Maybe we can bake some cookies when I get back."

Hannah Gruen was the Drews' housekeeper and had been like a mother to Nancy since Nancy's own mother had died when she was three.

"Cookies?" Mr. Drew laughed at his daughter. "When was the last time you had time to bake cookies?"

"I don't know," Nancy admitted. "But once this

case is solved, I'll have a little bit of free time before—"

"Before your next big case," Mr. Drew finished.
"Have fun, Nancy. Let me know if there's anything I can do for you."

"Thanks, Dad. I'll see you in a couple of days."
Nancy replaced the receiver and was startled
when the phone rang immediately.

"Hello?" she said breathlessly, glancing at her
watch. It was after ten o'clock.

"Hello. Is this Bess Marvin?" asked a female
voice, which Nancy recognized instantly as
Joyce's.

"No, Ms. Palmer. This is Nancy Drew. Would
you like to speak with Bess?"

"Please call me Joyce. And I'd like to speak
with both of you—but not over the phone. Do
you think you could come to my office to see
me?"

Nancy caught Bess's eye. "Sure," she said.
"We'll have to work out a time with Andrea,
though. Our schedule tomorrow is kind of
packed."

"Actually, I was hoping you could come right
now. It's vital that I talk to you immediately."

5

Battle Royal

"At this hour? Joyce wants us to go back to her office now?" Bess winced as she shoved her feet into her shoes. "She obviously has no idea what kind of day we've had."

"Something weird is going on," Nancy said. "I got the impression Joyce didn't want anyone to know she's talking to us. And why is she working so late, anyway?"

"Well, I guess I can catch a baseball game, since you two won't be here to object." George leaned back against her pillow and flipped on the TV to a sports channel. "Let me know how it goes."

Although the rain had stopped, Nancy was surprised at the chill in the air when she and Bess stepped outside. "It feels like fall," she said.

"Kings Commons will close for the season in a few weeks," Bess observed. "I guess I won't be claiming my trip part of the prize until next year. If ever."

"I can't wait to hear what Joyce has to tell us," Nancy said.

Joyce met Nancy and Bess at the entrance to the Royal Chocolates building. "Thanks for coming over so late. I wouldn't have asked you if it wasn't important." She punched a code into the security keypad and ushered them inside.

"Do you usually keep such late hours?" Nancy asked.

"Sometimes," Joyce said. "It's been kind of crazy in our department lately." She pressed the elevator button. "We've all been edgy. I know it's no excuse, but I want to apologize for the way I treated you earlier today. I had just been chewed out by my boss. . . ."

"We heard," Bess said.

"I'm sure." Joyce grimaced. "I guess you can imagine how I felt when I saw your winning wrapper—the *second* winning wrapper. You see, I'm in charge of contest security. If someone finds a way to crack the system and cheat, then it's my fault. And that means Mr. Tumey has a perfect excuse to fire me."

Nancy wondered why Joyce would think Mr. Tumey was looking for a reason to fire her.

As they settled into chairs in Joyce's office, Nancy asked the question uppermost in her mind. "How exactly *do* you prevent contest fraud, Joyce?"

"Generally, that information is a closely guarded secret," Joyce said. "But since you are directly affected, I'll tell you this much. In these days of color printers and copiers, it's obviously not difficult to counterfeit a winning wrapper. Therefore, we assign a special code number to the genuine instant-win wrapper in order to prevent forgeries. The number is printed beneath the words *Grand Prize*. Obviously, we guard the winning number with our lives. Only a handful of people at Royal have access to this information, and it's locked in a safe."

Nancy leaned forward. "And did Bess's wrapper have the correct code number?"

Joyce paused. "Yes. It certainly did. So far, your claim appears to be completely valid, Bess."

"But so does Diana's, I assume," Nancy said.

Joyce nodded. "That's right. The code number on her wrapper was also correct. And she's already been awarded the prize. Needless to say, Mr. Tumey is ready to have my head. The company can't afford to pay two winners. And this promotion has already cost Royal a lot of money. I'm afraid I'm going to lose my job."

Bess cleared her throat. "We're sorry to hear that, of course. But that can't be the reason you called us here at this hour."

"No. I talked to Mr. Tumey," Joyce explained. "We agreed that we can't afford the publicity that would be caused by bringing in the police at this point. But we need to get to the bottom of this mystery. We know you're a detective, Nancy, and we were wondering if you could help us."

"This whole scenario is very interesting." Nancy tapped her fingers on the desk. "Frankly, I don't understand why you'd come to me for help. I mean, earlier this afternoon you said you thought Bess might have cheated to win the contest. How do you know you can trust us?"

"It's not much of a risk," Joyce said with a smile. "I checked you out online and found old newspaper accounts of some of your cases. You're a bit of a celebrity, Nancy Drew. The River Heights police chief speaks highly of you—and your friends. So I think I can trust you and Bess. I *hope* I can. You're going to be investigating on your own regardless of what I say, right?"

"You'd better believe it," Bess replied.

Joyce fixed her eyes on Nancy. "I'm sure you can understand why I'd rather have you on our side than against us. And by working together, I'm sure we stand a much better chance of uncovering the truth. That's what we all want, isn't it?"

"Of course it is," Nancy agreed.

"Then you'll do it?" Joyce asked.

Nancy nodded.

"Thank you, thank you, thank you!" Joyce shook Nancy's hand. "I can't tell you how grateful I am. And, Bess—your patience will be rewarded. You have my word that this will all be straightened out very shortly."

"If Nancy's on the case, I'm sure it will," Bess said simply.

Joyce smiled. "I'm glad you have such confidence in your friend. Now, I know this is asking a lot, but if you could avoid contacting the media until the controversy is resolved, we would appreciate it. We're trying our best to keep this under wraps. We haven't even told Diana yet."

Nancy took a moment to digest this. Diana's earlier rudeness toward them would make a lot more sense if she knew she was competing with Bess for the contest money, but apparently she had no idea. "Why haven't you told Diana?"

"If she has committed fraud, we see no need to tip her off about the investigation. And the fewer people who know about the prize mix-up, the better from our point of view. If this contest turns into a public relations disaster, Pleasant Candies is sure to take an even bigger bite out of our business. Oh—" Joyce turned to Nancy. "Speaking of disasters, I understand that a crocodile nearly took a bite out of *you.*"

"I don't know how near it was," Nancy said, "but it wasn't exactly one of my trip highlights."

"Obviously, Royal Chocolates will pay for your extra night's motel stay. I also took the liberty of setting up a meeting between Andrea and the president of our company, Mr. Castle. You may not be aware that Royal awards a number of educational grants each year."

"I wasn't aware of that, but why would you assume Andrea would want to apply for one?"

"Nonprofit organizations can always use money, right? And Mr. Castle really likes to help worthy organizations, so I thought it might be worth a shot."

"It was kind of you to make arrangements for Andrea," Nancy said. "I'm sure she'll be grateful."

"Also," Joyce added, "I would imagine a tour of the chocolate factory is on your agenda."

Bess nodded. "Tomorrow morning."

"How would you like a personal tour guide to give you the inside scoop?"

"Free samples for everyone?" Bess asked.

Joyce laughed. "Definitely."

"You're on." Bess caught herself. "Wait a second. I'd better not get carried away. Andrea's in charge. Can we have her give you a call in the morning?"

"Sure," Joyce said. "I'll be here at seven."

"Yikes," Bess murmured to Nancy as they left Joyce's office. "I always thought working in a chocolate factory would be fun until I heard about Joyce's job."

Nancy nodded. "And I thought being a *detective* was stressful."

The next morning Nancy was pulling on a sweatshirt when Bess opened her eyes. "Please tell me it isn't morning already."

"Eight A.M. Rise and shine," Nancy said cheerfully.

Bess buried her face in her pillow. "Go away."

"I am," Nancy said. "But you'd better get up. Andrea arranged the factory tour for ten o'clock. And you've got a breakfast date with ten Sleuths."

Bess squinted at Nancy. "Where are you going?"

"The computer lab here at the Royal Museum. I spoke to Joyce this morning, and she says they have Internet access. I'm going to see what I can find out about Diana and Phil online."

"Aren't you going to eat breakfast?"

"I'll grab something later," Nancy said. "And

George will be back. She just went for a jog. I'll see you guys at the chocolate factory."

Nancy glanced at her Kings Commons map as she walked along the beautifully landscaped path called El Camino Real. She remembered from her Spanish classes that that meant "The Royal Way." The air was clear and crisp after the previous day's rain. Empty cars ran on Royal Pain's purple tracks, and the warm smell of chocolate hung over Kings Commons.

George jogged past Nancy. "Great day, isn't it?"

Nancy grinned. "I hope so."

The computer proctor stood up quickly when Nancy entered. He seemed surprised to see her. "Hi, I'm Stan. Can I help you?"

Nancy shook his hand. "My name's Nancy Drew. I was just hoping to get online."

"No problem." Stan led her to the nearest terminal. "Let me show you how to maneuver our Internet browser." He used the mouse to open the Royal Chocolates home page as an example. "If you want to perform a search, you click here." He demonstrated. "And if you want to go back to a recent search, you can click on the history button, like so. That way you can see—"

"Wait!" Nancy cried. She put a hand on the mouse. "When you clicked the history button, I thought I saw . . ." She repeated Stan's motions and took a close look at the name that had flashed on the screen a moment earlier. "Does this mean what I think it means?" she asked Stan.

Stan's brow furrowed as he read the screen. "This is strange. It looks like the last person who used this computer to search for information was looking for information about you!"

6

Jelly Rogers

Nancy looked at the keywords for the last several computer searches. "Nancy Drew," "Andrea Cassella," "Bess Marvin," "Science Sleuths." What could this mean? she asked herself. Who was searching for information about her and her friends?

"Do you have any idea who used this computer last?" Nancy asked Stan.

Stan shook his head. "Sorry. I just got in this morning, so this must have happened yesterday. Patsy was working then." He glanced at the schedule taped to the wall behind his desk. "You'll have to come back Wednesday—oh, that's tomorrow. Come back tomorrow and talk to her. But I'm afraid we get about three hundred users a day, and we don't have any sort of sign-up system for the users. I wouldn't bet that she'd remember."

"Okay. Thanks, Stan. You've been very helpful." Nancy gripped the mouse. "I think I can take it from here."

"Yell if you need anything," Stan said. He returned to his own work.

Nancy stared at the blue screen for a moment. She remembered Joyce's saying she'd performed an online search for information about Nancy and her cases. Surely she'd used the computer in her own office, and she hadn't mentioned looking up Andrea or the Sleuths. If someone else was investigating them, who could it be? She sighed as she looked at her watch—it was getting late. She'd better get on with her original plan.

She typed in Diana's name as the keyword for a new search. "Twenty-four hits," she read as the computer returned the results. That meant there were twenty-four mentions of Diana Nugent on the World Wide Web.

She pulled up the first match, which listed finish times for a recent California 5K race. The Diana Nugent mentioned had placed second in the eighteen-and-under category. "Definitely not our Diana," Nancy murmured. She bit her lip as, one by one, she discarded the entries returned by the search engine.

"Is everything going okay over there?" Stan asked.

"Mmm," Nancy murmured. She clicked on the seventeenth link. "I think . . ." She straightened up in her seat. "It might be going better now."

Finally she appeared to have uncovered something useful. Here was a web page for Gold Nugget Publishing, which listed Diana Nugent as its president and Phil Nugent as vice-president. Based on the conversation she'd heard earlier between Diana and Phil, Nancy realized this had to be their company. Publishing, she thought to herself. If Diana had high-quality printing equipment and the expertise, she would have the ability to forge a winning chocolate wrapper. That still left the problem of the code number. Diana's wrapper had had the correct instant-win code. How could she have gotten that information? Nancy wondered.

She skimmed through the various areas of the company's website—history, services offered, clients. Suddenly Nancy drew in her breath.

One of Gold Nugget's clients was Pleasant Candies! There was even a quote from Pleasant's president, Maggie Fitzwilliam, praising Diana's work. Could the fact that Pleasant Candies was their client possibly be a coincidence? Nancy asked herself. Could Diana be a link to the corporate spy?

A group of noisy students entered the lab at that moment, and Nancy realized someone would want to use her terminal. I'll just take five more minutes, she thought to herself, glancing at the clock on the computer screen.

"Oh, no," she whispered. It was already ten o'clock. She was late.

"Thanks for everything," she told Stan as she stuffed her pen and notebook into her bag and slung it over her shoulder. "I'll be back."

The chocolate factory was a short walk from the computer lab. Nancy found she didn't even need to check her map to orient herself; she could follow her nose.

She caught up with the Sleuths as Joyce was handing out cacao beans.

"Besides making chocolate, the ancient Aztecs used the cacao bean as a unit of currency," Joyce was explaining.

"Great. I hope they don't try to pay me my prize money in beans," Bess whispered to George.

Kenny bit into his and immediately made a face. "It tastes terrible." He spat it into a tissue Andrea handed him.

Joyce laughed. "I was about to tell you that you might not want to taste it. It's bitter because sugar hasn't been added to it."

Laura nodded. "I tasted my mother's baking chocolate once. It was gross."

"Let's go see what happens to the cacao beans after they've been roasted and blended." Joyce led the Sleuths into the next room. "We'll have better-tasting samples soon. I promise."

"Did I miss anything?" Nancy asked.

"Not really. I called to check on the van," Andrea said. "They still have no idea when it will be ready."

Nancy shook her head. "That's too bad." She nodded toward the Sleuths. "The kids seem to be enjoying the tour."

Andrea smiled. "Yes. Joyce is wonderful with them."

"I'm sorry I was late." Nancy glanced at the clear tubes, running from ceiling to floor, filled with a stream of melted chocolate that had been poured into them from huge vats on the second floor. She had never seen so much chocolate.

"You're never late without a good reason," Bess said to Nancy. "So spill the beans." She giggled. "No pun intended."

"I did learn something interesting," Nancy said. "Diana and Phil own a publishing company. And one of their clients *happens* to be Pleasant Candies."

"Wow," George said. "That would make it easy for them to print a fake wrapper."

"That's true," Andrea said. "But lots of people could probably do that. The question is, how would they get the right instant-win code?"

Bess nodded. "And what about Pleasant Candies? I don't understand why it's important."

"It's not as though anyone at Pleasant would know anything about Royal's contest," Andrea observed.

"Not necessarily," Nancy said quietly. She explained what she and Bess had overheard in Joyce's office about the possibility of a corporate spy at Royal.

"So," George said, "if somebody who worked for Pleasant came to Royal and nosed around looking for company secrets . . ."

"And found some—like the instant-win code, for instance," Bess said, getting the connection now. "If Diana has connections to Pleasant, maybe she was working with that employee and maybe he or she gave her the code number."

"Don't get too excited," Nancy cautioned Bess. "We don't have any proof. It's just an idea. In fact, I'm not even going to mention it to Joyce yet. I want to learn more about Diana's ties to Pleasant first."

Nancy stopped talking as she realized Joyce was asking the Sleuths a question.

"And who can guess why he decided to name the company Royal Chocolates?"

Katie's hand shot in the air. "Because his last name was Castle."

"Very good. Of course, that wasn't his real last

name. He changed it when he came over from Italy, so that it would sound more American. In the 1920s, people were not so tolerant of immigrants."

"Did he change his name back once he got rich and famous and successful?" Emma asked.

"That's a good question." Joyce paused. "No, Mr. Castle didn't change his name back, but he never forgot what it was like to be poor or to struggle. That's why it was so important to him that Royal Chocolates do things to help the community. He built a museum and an amusement park to provide safe and wholesome entertainment for the families of his employees.

"The current president of the company, Robert Castle the third, has continued in his grandfather's footsteps. Royal Chocolates remains active in community activities. We award scholarships and administer educational programs throughout the country."

Nancy heard footsteps behind her and turned to see a man striding toward them.

"Joyce," he said, his voice stern and clipped.

Joyce stopped talking midsentence. "Mr. Tumey."

John Tumey didn't seem to notice the Science Sleuths or the fact that Joyce was in the middle of something.

"We've got a crisis upstairs," he said. "I've been paging you for twenty minutes."

"I'm sorry," Joyce said. "I left my beeper in my office."

"Just where it belongs," John Tumey said sarcastically. "Where *you* belong, I might add."

Joyce took a deep breath. "I'll be back to work as soon as I'm finished here," she said firmly, swallowing the nervousness in her voice. "This is a public relations matter, and I did clear it with Mr. Castle."

"Yes," John said. "Imagine my surprise when he told me I'd find you here. I took the liberty of scheduling a conference call for you at ten-thirty with Toni Conte. Be there."

John stalked out before Joyce could reply.

Nancy noticed Joyce's flushed cheeks as she apologized to the Sleuths for the interruption.

"Now, where was I?"

"You were telling us how the air gets knocked out of the chocolates," Noah volunteered.

Joyce gestured toward the conveyor belt. "Yes. You can see the bumpy ride that's in store for the molded chocolate bars."

She showed the Sleuths how the candies bounced down the length of the room before disappearing into a metal tunnel.

"At this point, the chocolate is a hot liquid. It can reach temperatures of a hundred and fifty degrees Fahrenheit or more. How do you think we make it turn solid?"

"You cool it," several Sleuths answered.

"Excellent," Joyce said. "You're exactly right." She patted the metal tubing. "This is called the cooling tunnel. It's where the chocolate solidifies, before it reaches the inspectors. As you can probably guess, it's the inspectors' job to remove any bars which haven't molded perfectly."

Laura's hand waved in the air. "What do they do with those?"

"They can eat them. Or take them home to friends and family." Joyce smiled. "Sounds great, right? But most inspectors learn to control their appetites pretty quickly. Believe it or not, it's easy to get sick of chocolate."

"I can't believe it," Bess said to Nancy and George.

"These workers are making Jelly Rogers." Joyce gestured toward the production line as they passed. "It's a new candy that will be sold on a trial basis in three cities before the end of the year. How would you like to do a taste test?"

There was an enthusiastic chorus of yeses from the Sleuths and Bess.

"What are these?" Nancy asked as she and Andrea helped pass out the candies.

"Raspberry jellies covered with dark chocolate," Joyce said. "They're delicious. Not that I'm biased or anything."

Joyce asked the Sleuths to rate the candy on a

scale of one to ten in terms of flavor, texture, and overall appeal.

"Chocolate and fruit." Kenny made a face. "Zero."

"Hey. Let's not be rude. You know what Andrea would say," Bess chided him.

Surprised by Andrea's silence on the subject, Nancy turned to look for her. She was stunned to see Andrea seated on a bench, her face red, her breathing labored.

Nancy ran to her side. "Andrea. What's wrong?"

"I . . ." Andrea grasped Nancy's hand. "Help me!"

7

Paying Peanuts

"What is it? What can I do?" Nancy checked Andrea's pulse, which was rapid and weak.

Andrea lowered her head as though she were dizzy. "Allergic reaction," she managed to say.

Nancy knew Andrea carried medication in the Sleuths' first aid kit in case she had a life-threatening reaction. She pulled out the bag and dug through it until she found the syringe.

George glanced over at Nancy and saw what was happening. "Okay, everyone. Let's go to the gift shop," she said to the Sleuths abruptly.

"But—" Kenny protested.

"Let's go," George repeated. She shepherded

the group out of the room as Joyce and Bess hurried over to help Nancy with Andrea.

With her hand shaking, Andrea plunged the needle into her arm.

"What's wrong?" Joyce asked.

Nancy shook her head. "She's having an allergic reaction of some sort. I don't know. Please call nine-one-one."

Joyce nodded, already moving toward the door. "We have a nurse here. I'll go get her."

Nancy and Bess tried to make Andrea comfortable as they waited for help. Her breathing had improved following the injection.

"The peanut butter," Andrea whispered.

"Don't try to talk," Nancy said.

Andrea nodded and closed her eyes.

"Peanut butter?" Bess turned to Nancy. "I know Andrea's allergic to peanuts, but there's no peanut butter in Jelly Rogers."

"And that's what she was eating right before she got sick." Nancy spotted the torn Jelly Rogers wrapper on the bench next to Andrea. Two candies were packaged together, but only one remained in the wrapper. "We'll give this to the paramedics." Nancy began wrapping the uneaten chocolate. "They can have it analyzed at the hospital lab."

Bess cast an expert glance at the candy in Nancy's hands. "There's no need," she said.

"That's not a Jelly Roger. It looks almost the same, but do you see the crimped edges? It's a Kings Cup."

Bess took the chocolate from Nancy and broke it open to prove her point. It was filled with crumbly peanut butter.

Nancy raised her head when she heard Joyce running toward them with a young woman in uniform. "The paramedics are on the way. Is she okay?"

"I think so." Nancy stepped away to give the nurse room to examine Andrea. The paramedics arrived within a few minutes and administered oxygen as they prepared to transport Andrea to the hospital.

"She's going to be fine," the nurse assured Joyce. "They'll probably keep her overnight for observation, but there should be no lasting effects."

Joyce gave a sigh of relief. "At last, some good news." Then she noticed the candy Bess was holding. "Where did you get that?"

"This was wrapped in the Jelly Roger package Andrea was given," Nancy explained. "Apparently, she got a Kings Cup by accident."

Joyce's hand went to her mouth. "Are you saying the wrapper was mislabeled?"

"Yes," Bess said. "And Andrea's allergic to peanuts, so . . ."

"So," Joyce finished, "we're lucky this turned out as well as it did. Not only for Andrea. Life-threatening allergies to peanuts aren't uncommon. If these candies had gone out to stores this way, people might have *died* because of our mistake." She took the Kings Cup from Bess. "I'll have to tell the workers to stop production, and then pull all the batches that have already been packaged. That's the only way to make sure no one else gets sick."

Joyce left to find the factory supervisor as the paramedics bundled Andrea onto the gurney to wheel her out.

Nancy and Bess found George in the gift shop, waiting for the Sleuths to move through the line with their chocolate purchases.

"Is Andrea okay?" George asked as soon as she caught sight of her friends.

"The paramedics took her to the hospital," Nancy said. "They think she'll be fine."

"That's a relief. What happened?" George wanted to know.

Bess explained about the Kings Cup mix-up.

"Mix-up?" George asked. "Or deliberate attempt to hurt Andrea?"

"But who could benefit from having Andrea out of the way?" Nancy asked. "I'll admit, the thought did cross my mind, but who knew about Andrea's allergy besides us? Diana, I guess. I don't see how she could have been involved in switching Andrea's candy sample. And, as I said, why would she want to hurt Andrea?"

"She might want to get *me* out of the way," Bess noted. "But not Andrea."

Nancy shook her head. "Actually, she doesn't know about your wrapper. And Royal is doing a thorough investigation of her right now. If she cheated, she's out of luck regardless of whether someone else comes forward to claim the prize."

"So you're saying what happened to Andrea was a coincidence," George said. "An accident."

"No." Nancy glanced toward the Sleuths. "Since we got here yesterday, we've had two unfortunate accidents and one piece of incredibly good luck. I don't think any of it could be called coincidence."

Nancy went on to explain about what she had discovered in the computer lab about someone searching for information about their group.

Bess tapped her foot. "I don't get it. Who would do that? Why?"

Nancy shrugged. "Aside from the instant-win wrapper, we're just an ordinary group visiting Kings Commons. And no one knows about the instant-win wrapper, so I'm totally baffled, too," Nancy admitted.

"Totally baffled?" Joyce came up behind them

and put a hand on Nancy's shoulder. "That's great. Me, too."

"Did you get the factory to pull the Kings Cups?" Nancy asked.

"Yes," Joyce said, "but now we've got a new situation. I'm glad I tracked you down. I have to get back to my office, but I wanted to let you know. The Royal lab finished the chemical analysis of Bess's wrapper. It showed traces of rubber cement, which did not come from the Royal Chocolates factory."

"I don't understand," Bess said. "What does rubber cement have to do with anything?"

"I don't understand, either," Joyce replied. "I was hoping you might be able to give us some idea as to how it came to be found there and why."

"Uh—n-no," Bess stammered. "I guess we could ask Andrea about it. Once she's feeling better."

"There's another problem, too. I had scheduled Andrea for a meeting with Mr. Castle this morning about an educational grant. She's obviously not going to be able to make it. Mr. Castle is booked solid the rest of the week, so we can't postpone. What do you want me to do?"

Nancy thought for a moment. "I hope Andrea won't mind, but would it be okay if I met with Mr. Castle?"

Joyce brightened. "That's a great idea. Mr. Castle was only told he'd be meeting with a representative from the Science Sleuths. So why not you."

Joyce told Nancy to report to the fifth floor at eleven-fifteen and to wait for her in the reception area. "I've got to run," she said. "I'll see you there."

Bess turned to Nancy as Joyce hurried off. "Okay, Nan. What's going on here? Rubber cement?"

"It's all very strange," Nancy agreed, "and it keeps getting stranger." She unzipped her purse. "I'm glad I stashed away this Crown Jewels bar for an emergency. I knew I shouldn't have skipped breakfast." She began to tear the wrapper, then stopped suddenly.

"What's the matter, Nan?" George asked.

"Do you see anything unusual here?" Nancy held up the wrapper.

George looked at Nancy. "Do you mean besides the fact that you're eating chocolate for breakfast?"

"This is the Crown Jewels bar Andrea gave me yesterday," Nancy said. "The one she bought in River Heights along with Bess's."

"Wait a minute," Bess said. "That wrapper doesn't say anything about an instant win contest."

"Exactly," Nancy said. "We know they're not

selling the instant-win bars at Kings Commons. Therefore, we know your winning bar came from outside the park, Bess. The others—or at least this one—clearly came from somewhere else. Probably one of the vendors right here."

"I don't understand." Bess sank into a chair. "Why would Andrea lie to us?"

8

Making Waves

Before Nancy could answer, the Sleuths took off. They raced out of the gift shop with their bags of Royal merchandise.

"We're not going to hang out here all day, are we?" Kenny asked. "I want to go on some rides."

"We will," Bess promised.

"I thought we were going to the water park," Emma said.

"We are," Bess assured her.

"I'm hungry," Noah complained.

"I know, I know, I know. We'll get a snack first, then go to the water park, then on to the rides." Bess ticked off the agenda on her fingers. "Any complaints? Wait! On second thought, don't answer that question."

Nancy grinned at George. "I think you guys have everything under control. I hope you don't mind if I duck out, but I've got to take care of a few things before I see Mr. Castle."

George waved her hand. "No problem. We should be fine until the water park. At which point we'll need you desperately."

Nancy nodded. "I'll meet you there."

Nancy went back to the motel room. First things first, she told herself inside her room. She picked up the phone and called the hospital to check on Andrea.

Andrea's condition was good, the nurse reported, and she should be released in the morning. However, she was asleep and could not speak with Nancy right then.

Nancy sighed. Now might not be the time to bring up the rubber cement, but she had really hoped to discuss the Science Sleuths program with Andrea before she met with Mr. Castle. Nancy looked down at her sweatshirt and faded jeans—she needed to change into something more presentable. She raided Bess's side of the closet for a navy blazer. It was a little large, but it would have to do.

Next she put on a clean pair of khakis and finally dug around in her suitcase for the brochures

Andrea had given her about the Science Sleuths. After reviewing them, she felt better prepared for her meeting with Mr. Castle. If he asked any tough questions, she'd have to get the answers from Andrea later, she told herself.

Joyce buzzed Nancy into the building and was waiting for her in the fifth floor reception area at eleven-fifteen on the dot.

"I'll take you in and introduce you to Mr. Castle," Joyce said. "But first, let me offer a word of advice. As you might imagine, the whole instant-win disaster is a very touchy subject with Mr. Castle. He doesn't know you have any connection to Bess, and you'll probably want to keep it that way."

"That makes sense," Nancy agreed. "Thanks for the tip."

Joyce knocked timidly on the door before ushering Nancy into an enormous suite at the end of the hall.

Joyce cleared her throat. "Mr. Castle," she said softly, "this is Nancy Drew of the Science Sleuths in River Heights. She's here to speak with you about applying for an educational grant."

Mr. Castle rose and shook Nancy's hand. He was at least six feet four, Nancy guessed. She had to crane her neck to meet his gaze. He wore an expensive-looking suit, and his sideburns were tinged with gray. "Pleased to meet you, Ms. Drew," he greeted her.

"Likewise," Nancy said, taking the seat he offered her. "Please, call me Nancy."

"Good luck," Joyce mouthed to Nancy as she pulled the door closed behind her.

"Thank you for taking the time to meet with me," Nancy said.

The corners of his eyes crinkled as Mr. Castle smiled. "It's always a pleasure to help a worthy cause," he told Nancy. "Joyce says the Science Sleuths are here at Kings Commons for an educational field trip. Perhaps you could tell me a little about the work that you do."

Nancy gave a brief explanation of the group's mission and activities. Mr. Castle nodded encouragingly as she explained how the park's rides, the wildlife, and the chocolate factory fit into their lesson plans for the week.

"I'm impressed," he said when Nancy paused to take a breath.

"I'm sorry I can't give you more details," Nancy apologized. "The leader of our group, Andrea Cassella, was supposed to meet with you this morning, but she was indisposed and I was asked to fill in at the last minute."

Mr. Castle fumbled with his pen, his expression suddenly very serious.

"Pardon me. What did you say?"

"I said our leader was indisposed—"

"What happened to her?" Mr. Castle interrupted, his voice impatient.

Nancy wiped her palms on Bess's blazer. She wasn't sure what had happened, but this interview had definitely taken a turn for the worse.

Nancy cleared her throat. "Andrea has a peanut allergy. On the factory tour, she accidentally ate a peanut butter candy and had to be taken to the emergency room."

"Accidentally?" Mr. Castle pronounced each syllable distinctly. "How, exactly, did that happen?"

Nancy explained that the candy wrapper was mislabeled.

"Ah, yes." Mr. Castle nodded. "The two hundred thousand dollar mistake. We were forced to stop production of our Jelly Rogers candies and pull all those currently scheduled for shipment. All because of your friend's *accident*."

Was Mr. Castle implying that it wasn't an accident? Surely he couldn't blame Andrea for what had happened, Nancy thought. Could he? "It certainly was unfortunate," Nancy agreed, "but I'm afraid I don't understand—"

"Frankly, Ms. Drew," Mr. Castle interrupted, "Royal Chocolates is having a disastrous year financially. A competitor has introduced a rival candy which has decreased our profits dramatically. With the additional burden of today's Jelly

Rogers recall—the one in which your friend was involved—I'm sorry to say that I've decided to suspend our educational grants program. Effective immediately."

Nancy relaxed her head against the chair's high back. She didn't understand what had just happened. Mr. Castle was acting as though Andrea had gotten sick on purpose. As though she had actually set out to hurt Royal's business.

At the beginning of their conversation, Mr. Castle had seemed interested in the Sleuths' program and willing to help. Yet now he was saying that the entire educational grants program was to be discontinued.

Before she could decide how to phrase an appeal, Mr. Castle stood, clearly ready to end their interview.

"I'm sorry to have wasted your time," he said. "If there are any changes in the status of the program, I'll let your friend—Ms. Cassella?—know."

Nancy nodded, aware of the tension in the man's voice as he said Andrea's name.

"I'll let Ms. Cassella know. Now, if you'll excuse me—" He escorted Nancy to the door.

Nancy handed him the Science Sleuths brochures that she had tucked into her purse. "I sympathize with your difficulties, Mr. Castle, but I hope you will keep us in mind if funds do become available. I'd like to leave these with you.

They describe the Science Sleuths' program, and we would appreciate it if you'd review them at your convenience." She shook his hand. "Thank you for your time."

Nancy found Joyce on the phone in her office. Joyce held up a hand and motioned for Nancy to sit while she quickly wrapped up her conversation.

"What happened?" Joyce put a hand over Nancy's as she hung up the receiver. "You look as though you've been through the wringer."

"Our meeting didn't exactly go well," Nancy said. "Mr. Castle claims the educational grants program has been canceled."

Joyce's brown eyes widened. "Really? I'm surprised. I am sorry, Nancy, but please don't take it personally. Mr. Castle is famous for his whims. I bet he changed his mind after we pulled that batch of Jelly Rogers today. The company lost a lot of money, and he's very upset."

Nancy nodded. She was sure there was more to it than that, but she didn't want to get into it with Joyce.

"While we're on the subject of our company's sad finances," Joyce said, "have you managed to come up with anything on Diana?"

Nancy shook her head. "I'm following a few leads, but I don't have anything solid yet. Can I call you later to discuss what I'm working on?"

"Sure. Whenever." Joyce slumped down in her seat. "I'll be here."

Nancy glanced at her watch. "Oh, boy, I've got to get going. Bess and George will be having their hands full at the water park."

Joyce smiled. "I'll say. You go ahead. We'll talk later. And please send Andrea my best."

"I will. Thanks." As Nancy stepped out of the office she practically mowed down John Tumey.

"Pardon me," he said, moving quickly out of her way.

Nancy noticed his downcast eyes and his jumpy demeanor. He had obviously been eavesdropping, Nancy realized. Why would he care what she had to say to Joyce? There was only one thing she knew for certain, she decided. Royal Chocolates was one strange place.

So was Water Wonderland, where Nancy found the Sleuths beside a pool cluttered with flip-flops and towels and people. Kings Commons seemed a world away. Rather than chocolate, the air smelled of chlorine. Speakers blared perky carousel music.

"If I hear 'Row, Row, Row Your Boat' one more time . . ." Bess murmured through clenched teeth. "Oh, Nan, what happened?"

Before Nancy could answer Kenny tugged on Bess's arm. "I forgot my towel," he said.

"That's no problem. We can rent one for the outrageous fee of two dollars." Bess inserted quarters into a machine in rapid succession. "Voilà," she said. "One towel. What I want to know is, how can Royal have financial troubles with prices like these?"

"I don't know, but you wouldn't believe the troubles they do have," Nancy told her. "Mr. Castle decided to cancel the educational grants program today."

"You're kidding," Bess said, handing Emma her flip-flops. "Why did he agree to meet with you in the first place?"

Nancy shrugged. "If you ask me, the whole thing is very fishy."

Kenny whipped his towel through the air. "Will we be seeing any little fishies in the Royal Wave pool?"

Nancy laughed. "Is that a hint, Kenny?"

"Yes. I'm ready to go swimming."

"So are we. Come on. Let's go." George hustled the Sleuths toward the wave pool.

Glistening water stretched in every direction. Blue waves lapped against a sandy shore dotted with colorful beach towels. In the middle of the Royal Wave pool stood a tall ship with water slides and gangplanks for diving.

"We're going on Her Majesty's Ship," Emma announced.

"Wait." Bess stopped her before she took off running. "These are the rules. Stay with your buddy at all times. Listen to the lifeguards. No running. No cannonballs."

"Besides those," Laura said, pointing at the large cannons on the side of the ship.

"And Tyler and Katie, don't go in deeper than three feet," Bess said. "This is not the place to try to learn to swim."

Tyler saluted. "Aye, Captain."

The Sleuths giggled.

"No running!" Bess called after them as they took off for the water.

A few minutes later Nancy, Bess, and George were treading water in the deep area beside Her Majesty's Ship, trying to keep their eyes on all ten Sleuths.

"So what happened in Mr. Castle's office?" George asked.

Nancy gave Bess and George a brief summary. "The strangest part was that Mr. Castle's attitude changed as soon as he heard Andrea's name. It was almost as though he knew her."

"But of course he doesn't," Bess said, her breath coming in gasps as she struggled to keep her head above the water. "Know her, I mean. Andrea would have told us."

"I hope so," Nancy said. "But Mr. Castle was so suspicious, Bess. In fact, he practically accused her of having an allergic reaction on purpose."

"As if she would almost die on purpose," Bess scoffed.

George pushed dark, wet ringlets of hair from her eyes. "I hate to say it, but Mr. Castle's idea might not be so out there. I mean, Andrea *is* the one who ate the peanut butter—even if it was an accident. She's the one who drove our van off the road—even if it was an accident. And she's the one who gave Bess that instant-win bar. . . ." George trailed off.

"Even if that was an accident?" Nancy asked. "Is that what you were going to say?"

"I don't know," George replied. "Andrea let us think she bought Bess's candy here at the park when she didn't. She told us she bought all the candy at once, when apparently she didn't. Also, how did Bess's wrapper get rubber cement on it? Unless Andrea put it there."

"But why would she do that?" Bess asked. "What would Andrea get out of any of this?"

"This is just a theory," Nancy said, "but Royal Chocolates and Mr. Castle have been hurt by every single thing that's happened to us. If—and it's a big if—if Andrea does actually have some sort of connection to Robert Castle, maybe she also had a way of getting the instant-win code from Royal. It's a long shot, I know." Nancy spoke slowly, choosing her words with care. "But it's not inconceivable that Andrea's the one who counterfeited the winning wrapper."

"Then stuck it together with the rubber cement," George said.

Bess's jaw dropped and water ran into her mouth. "That doesn't make any sense," she sputtered. "If she made herself an instant-win wrapper, why did she turn around and give it to me?"

"It must have been a mistake," George said dismissively. "She got the chocolate bars mixed up."

Nancy kicked onto her back and floated. "That's possible, I guess. But nothing adds up. We can't leap to conclusions, and we definitely have to talk to Andrea."

"Watch me!" Laura called. She bounced on the end of the gangplank, then did a quick somersault. Toes pointed, she landed a few feet from Nancy's head.

Nancy choked as waves washed over her face. She lifted her head and looked toward the shallow end. Her heart went to her throat. Katie and Tyler were gone.

9

Deepening and Darkening

"Katie!" Bess called. "Katie! Tyler!"

"They were just there a second ago." George's powerful crawl stroke had already propelled her halfway to the shallow end.

Nancy turned to the lifeguard, who shouted at Nancy, "Do they know how to swim?"

Nancy shook her head grimly as she got out of the pool. Just then she saw Katie's head pop out from behind the lifeguard tower. Her wet feet slapped against the pavement as she and Tyler both hurried toward Nancy.

The guard blew her whistle at them. "No running!"

"These are the children," Nancy said to the guard. "They're here!" she called, waving her arms at Bess and George.

"No running!" the lifeguard yelled as Bess raced toward them. George followed a few steps behind.

"Don't you know you can't disappear like that?" Bess scolded, keeping one eye on the other Sleuths and the tall ship.

"Sorry," Katie said, her eyes downcast.

"What do you think you were doing?" Bess demanded.

"Someone was spying on us," Tyler said.

"We saw her. Over there." Katie pointed behind the lifeguard tower. "But her face was all covered up with a floppy flowered hat and sunglasses."

"We tried to catch her, but she got away. Look—we found a clue. Besides being a spy, she's also a litterbug. She dropped this." Tyler held up a Crown Jewels wrapper. "It must have been that Diana lady who hates us. She's always eating these chocolates, and she's always following us wherever we go."

"Tyler, I don't mean to criticize your detective work," Bess said, "but we're at Royal Chocolates headquarters. *Everyone's* eating these Crown Jewels bars."

"Wait a minute," Nancy said to Tyler and Katie.

"I know you guys are good observers. Did you notice the woman's legs?"

"Yes," Katie said. "She had a bruise on her knee. It was really big and purple."

Nancy turned to Bess and George. "I remember Diana complaining that she had bruised her leg yesterday. I know lots of people have bruises on their legs, but Tyler and Katie are right. Diana does seem to be following us wherever we go. Why is that?"

"Hey!" George shouted at Kenny and Noah. "Stop splashing."

"But we're doing an experiment," Kenny said.

"Splash equals mass times acceleration," Noah called out. "One, two, three. Go!"

"Great. A contest to see who can splash the hardest," Bess said. "Okay!" she yelled. "Out of the water. Everybody out."

"But we're not finished," Noah said.

"I didn't get to go on the water slide on my back," Emma complained. "Only my stomach. I won't be able to compare the velocities for my assignment."

Bess held up her hands. "We're all turning into wrinkled prunes, and Laura's lips are blue. It's time to get out of the water. I'm sorry."

"Don't mess with Bess," Katie said to Ashley. Nancy smiled as Ashley nodded solemnly.

"I heard that," Bess said. Then she grinned, and the girls burst into giggles.

After changing back into their street clothes, the Sleuths waited in line at the gate to return to the main park.

"Hey!" Kenny shouted.

Bess jumped. "Kenny, you scared me half to death—" she began.

"Hey!" Kenny shouted louder. "There's that Diana lady."

Nancy spotted Diana coming through the gate that led into the water park. She looked up when she heard her name.

"How come you were spying on us when we were swimming?" Kenny asked her. "Don't you know that's rude?"

Diana turned to her husband, ignoring Kenny. "I wish those kids would leave us alone," Nancy heard her say. "I don't know what he's talking about. I haven't been to the water park today."

She shoved through the crowd, and she and Phil disappeared inside the park.

Kenny made his way over to Nancy. "Diana's lying," Kenny said proudly. "I saw her hand. It had a whale stamp on it. That means she was already inside the water park. She was inside and then left."

"Great detective work, Kenny," Nancy praised him.

"How's this for detective work?" Kenny asked. "I see Royal Pain is running again." He pointed off into the distance. "Therefore, I deduce that it must be fixed. Can we go on it now?"

"Please? Pretty please?" the rest of the Sleuths chorused.

"Sure," George said.

Bess shot her cousin a look. "I'm not going on that thing," she whispered fiercely.

George laughed. "After our kiddie coaster experience, I think that's probably a good idea."

"Anyone who doesn't want to go on Royal Pain can come with me," Bess said. "Instead, we'll go to . . ."

"The haunted house!" Laura shouted.

Nancy glanced at her map. "That would be Castle Ballyboo. We'll all walk this way, then you go north."

As they got closer to Royal Pain, Kenny's eyes grew wide. "I didn't realize it was so . . ."

"Big and scary looking," Emma said as a car zipped overhead, the shrieks of its riders hanging in the air.

"I'm not going on that," Ashley said. "No, thanks."

"Raise your hand if you're going on Royal Pain with me," George asked.

"Well, I guess I'll go to the haunted castle with

you," Nancy told Bess after she counted only two hands. They left George, Katie, and Noah at the roller coaster line, which snaked out of the waiting area, around the games booths, and back across the drawbridge.

"I bet we can do three rides in the time it takes them to ride Royal Pain," Bess said as they approached the castle door. "And we'll probably still get back to the motel first."

"This doesn't seem to be one of the park's more popular attractions," Nancy observed. There was no line at all. In fact, the entire area around the castle appeared to be deserted.

Nancy struggled with the heavy castle door, which creaked open reluctantly. She poked her head into the gray gloom. Cobwebs hung from the ceiling. A cold mist floated in the air.

A pair of eyes glowed red in the darkness, and organ music played in a minor key.

"This is so cheesy," Kenny said. He raced ahead of the group. "Fake bats, fake blood, fake screams."

"Kenny! Don't get too far ahead of us," Bess called.

Her voice echoed back to them, and she shivered. "It's cold in here. And I don't care what Kenny says—I think it's creepy."

They rounded a corner, and Bess paused to examine a corpse in a crumbling coffin. "Yuck."

Nancy walked ahead with Laura. "Are you coming?" she called back to Bess. "Bess?" she repeated.

The only answer she received was Bess's blood-curdling scream.

10

Touched by a Corpse

"Nancy!" Bess screamed. "Nan!"

Nancy raced back through the narrow passageway to the spot where she had left Bess.

Bess stood, frozen, as she pointed toward the coffin.

"That corpse. It touched me!"

Cackling laughter filled the air. Nancy felt her skin prickle as the "corpse" sat up and took a slow bow.

Nancy squinted into the darkness. "Kenny?"

Kenny jumped up and hit his head on the coffin's lid. "Ow."

"Serves you right," Bess murmured.

Kenny ducked under the wooden barrier that

separated the exhibit from the walking path for the public. "I got you good."

"You certainly did," Bess agreed. "That's two near heart attacks in the last hour thanks to you Sleuths. My quota for the day has been exceeded."

Nancy and Bess wound through the rest of the exhibit and found the other Sleuths staring at a glowing skeleton.

"Phosphorescence at work," Emma said. "Who would think the haunted house could be educational?"

"Speaking of educational," Bess said, "there's time for one ride before we go back to the motel so you can work on your journals." She turned to Nancy. "I need a nap," she whispered.

Nancy nodded. She was tired, too. The sun and the water had sapped her energy. So had the endless conversation with the Sleuths.

"You wouldn't believe the wild stuff I found in that coffin." Kenny held out his palm. "The back of somebody's earring. A pacifier. And somebody obviously didn't like those new Royal gumdrops."

"I certainly hope you're planning to wash your hands as soon as possible," Bess said.

"You're just grumpy because I scared you," Kenny replied.

"Practically to death," Bess agreed. "Do you want to see my name on one of those tombstones?"

"No," Kenny said. "But you'll never guess what name I *did* see on a grave back there."

Nancy held up her hands. "You're right. I'll never guess."

"Cassella," Kenny said. "You know—as in Andrea."

"Hmm." Nancy's steps slowed as she contemplated what Kenny had just said.

Bess caught Nancy's eye. "I see those wheels turning," she said quietly. "What are you thinking?"

"I was just wondering . . . I know this sounds ridiculous, but if there *is* a connection between Andrea and Robert Castle, could that tombstone have something to do with it?"

Bess made a face. "That's a pretty far-out idea. Yikes. I hope not."

"I hate to say it, but I hope *so*. I hope Kenny found us a clue. And I hope Andrea can offer us some kind of reasonable explanation for all of this."

After one more ride, Nancy and Bess helped the Sleuths settle in with their homework at the motel. Then Nancy called to check on the van. With any luck, she was told, it might be ready in the morning. Then she phoned the hospital, only to learn that Andrea was sleeping—again.

Nancy sighed. "An unconscious witness is not very helpful," she told Bess.

"Hey, what's that?" Bess asked, and bent down

to pick up a piece of paper that had been shoved under the front door. "The desk took a message for you, Nan. It's from your dad."

Nancy felt a twinge of fear. She knew her dad probably wouldn't call her unless it was important. She hoped nothing was wrong.

Her father picked up the phone on the first ring. "Nothing's wrong," he said immediately.

"That's good," Nancy said, relieved. "So what's going on?"

"Apparently, a woman called here earlier this afternoon asking several questions about you," Mr. Drew explained. "Hannah thought you should know. Also, could you please reassure her that you're not doing anything dangerous?"

"Sure." Nancy smiled as she waited for her father to hand over the phone. "I'm fine, Hannah. Don't worry about me."

"That's easy for you to say." Hannah chuckled.

"What did this woman ask you when she called?" Nancy asked.

"She said she was a reporter doing a story about one of your cases," Hannah said. "After she asked a few questions, I got a bit suspicious. And when I pressed her for details, she hung up."

"Hmm," Nancy said. "Is there anything else you can tell me about your conversation?"

"As a matter of fact," Hannah replied, "I noticed that there was a lot of noise in the background during the call. There were people shouting and laughing, and also some sort of tinny music. It was playing—"

" 'Row, Row, Row Your Boat?' " Nancy asked.

Hannah clicked her tongue. "Nancy Drew, how did you know that?"

Nancy laughed. "Just a hunch. Thanks, Hannah. You did great. And everything's under control here. I promise."

"What was that all about?" Bess asked as Nancy hung up the phone.

"It seems that someone called my house and tried to grill Hannah about me. It also seems that the call came from Water Wonderland."

"Diana?" Bess wondered.

"Well," Nancy said, "we know she was at the water park earlier today and seemed to be spying on us. We also know someone was doing research on us online in the computer lab. Was it the same person? Was it Diana? I don't know."

George breezed in just then, her short hair tousled and her cheeks pink. "That was an awesome ride. It was definitely worth the wait. We went on it twice."

"Did Katie and Noah love it?" Bess asked.

"Katie did. Noah said he'll let us know after his stomach settles."

"I hope you started them on their homework," Bess said.

George nodded. "Do you think I'd forget my chaperoning duties? Noah couldn't wait to interpret his data. He thinks Royal Pain is going to edge Labyrinth for the title of speed queen by a few centimeters per second."

There was a knock on the door.

"Come in!" Bess called.

The door opened a crack. "I'm sorry to bother you," Laura said. "I'm stuck on this problem. Can you help me?"

Nancy pursed her lips. "We're not exactly science experts," she said, "but we'll give it a try. What is it?"

"I got a little distracted during the chocolate factory tour," Laura explained, "when Andrea got sick. Have you talked to her?"

Nancy motioned for Laura to sit down. "I was going to make an announcement at dinner. Andrea was asleep when I called the hospital, so I didn't actually speak with her. But she's doing well. She should be released in the morning. And the van might be fixed, too."

Laura seemed relieved. "Thanks, Nancy. It makes me feel a lot better to know that."

"So," Bess said, "what's your problem with this worksheet?"

Laura pointed to several diagrams on the page. "If you have this many gallons of milk produced by this many cows, plus this much sugar cane, how many pounds of cacao beans do you need to make this much dark chocolate, milk chocolate, and cocoa butter?"

"Yikes," Bess said. "Who made up this problem?"

Nancy leafed through Laura's factory tour notes to find the proportions of ingredients in the different types of chocolate. With a little guidance, Laura was able to plug in the correct values and arrive at an answer.

Laura thanked Nancy for her help. She pressed her hand against her growling stomach. "Just thinking about all that chocolate makes me hungry."

"I'm hungry, too," Bess said. "Why don't you go back to your room and get ready for dinner? We'll be going in a few minutes."

"What are we eating tonight?" Laura asked.

"Italian," Bess replied. "Yum."

"Italian . . ." Nancy's voice trailed off.

"What?" George closed the door behind Laura. "You like Italian food, don't you?"

"No. I mean, yes, I do. I was just thinking. Joyce said that the founder of Royal Chocolates was an Italian immigrant who changed his name, right?"

"Mm-hmm." Bess ran a comb through her tangled hair. "And that has something to do with dinner?"

Nancy shook her head. "Do you know if Andrea's Italian, Bess?"

"I think so. Her name sounds Italian. Why?"

"The founder of Royal Chocolates changed his name to Castle. What if his original name was . . . Cassella?"

Bess gasped. "Are you saying . . . ? Those rich relatives of Andrea's?"

"The Castles?" George guessed.

"Maybe," Nancy said. "And maybe, when they weren't willing to take her calls about funding for the Sleuths, that made her angry."

"Angry enough to try to ruin their business?" George asked. "To crash the van and plan the allergy attack and make an extra instant-win wrapper?"

"Anger doesn't seem like a very strong motivation to go to all that trouble," Bess argued. "Besides, we don't have any proof—"

"I know," Nancy said. "I know it sounds crazy. But, Bess, I just realized. If Andrea really is related to Robert Castle, I think I know why she gave you the winning chocolate bar."

11

Theory of Relativity

"Do you remember those documents Joyce had you sign?" Nancy asked Bess. "You had to swear you weren't related to any employees of Royal Chocolates. If you were, you'd be ineligible to win a prize in the contest."

"I get it," George said. "That means if Andrea really is a Castle, she'd be disqualified if she tried to claim the grand prize."

"We know Andrea's desperate for money to keep the Science Sleuths going," Nancy said. "Maybe she hoped the Castles would donate the money. When they refused to meet with her or even hear her out, maybe she decided to go to plan B."

Bess raised her eyebrows. "Plan B?"

"You know," George said. "Forge the winning wrapper, give it to you, drop a hint about donating some of the money back to the Sleuths, and hope that you'd be nice enough to do it."

"Okay," Bess said, "I admit that that would explain the rubber cement. It would also explain why Andrea lied to us about where she got the chocolates. But it still doesn't convince me she could have forged a wrapper with the right instant-win code."

"I think I know how she did that, too." George held up a hand when Bess frowned. "Just listen, okay? We know everybody thinks there's a Pleasant Candies spy at Royal. If Andrea really does have a grudge against her Castle relatives, what better way to get back at them? Royal's had a disastrous year financially. And a spy who infiltrated the company could have found out the instant-win code, right? If Andrea was working with that spy to begin with . . ."

"That makes sense," Bess admitted.

"Whether Andrea's involved or not, I think we're on the right track." Nancy flipped open her address book. "We've made a lot of educated guesses with very little actual evidence. Proof is what we need now. And I think we'll find that when we find the Pleasant spy."

"Do you have any idea who the spy could be?" Bess nodded toward the book in Nancy's hands. "Is that who you're calling?"

"I wish." Nancy laughed. "Not only don't I know who it is, I don't know anything about the person. I don't know for sure that the spy was the one responsible for leaking the instant-win code. I don't know whether he or she knew Andrea, or Diana, or both. The only thing I do know is where to look for him—or her."

Bess inched forward in her chair. "You do?"

"Well," Nancy said, "the spy has to work for Royal Chocolates, right? We have a contact at Royal Chocolates: Joyce, who's also looking for this person. I say we pool our resources and see what we can find out."

Nancy picked up the phone and dialed Joyce's office number.

"I'm glad to hear from you," Joyce told Nancy when she picked up the phone. "Things are really tense around here. I hope you have some good news for me."

"Not exactly." Nancy explained that she had not been able to speak with Andrea yet. Nor had they been able to visit the hospital because the van was in the shop and because Andrea was asleep every time she'd phoned.

"What about Diana?" Joyce asked. "Did you dig up anything?"

"Maybe. Just out of curiosity," Nancy asked, "what did Diana tell you her occupation was?"

"Publishing," Joyce replied promptly. "Very interesting, I know. But if she got hold of the instant-win code, I don't know how. She doesn't have any connections to Royal that we can discover. I mean, besides her attempt to get work with us, which went nowhere."

"Wait a minute," Nancy said. "Diana tried to get a job at Royal?"

"Well, sort of. Her publishing company does promotional materials for a number of medium-size corporations. They tried to recruit us as new clients a few months ago. They do a nice job, but we have our own printers. Therefore, we had to decline her bid."

"How did she react?" Nancy asked.

"Oh, fine. She went out and got herself hired immediately by Pleasant Candies. If you haven't noticed, Diana has a true love affair with chocolate."

"I've noticed," Nancy said.

"So where do we go from here?" Joyce asked.

"Well, I was thinking we might try a new approach," Nancy said. "And I was hoping you might be able to help me."

"Anything I can do," Joyce said. "Any ideas would be greatly appreciated."

"I want to try to find the corporate spy," Nancy said.

"What? I mean, so do I. But what does that have to do with the instant-win contest?"

"I think it's possible that the spy leaked the instant-win code to the person who printed the fake wrapper. I know it sounds far-fetched, and I could be completely wrong, but it's important to find the spy regardless, right?"

"Right," Joyce agreed. "So how do you propose that we do that?"

"I was hoping you could give me access to official Royal files. Personnel records, et cetera."

Joyce hesitated. "If my bosses found out, I'd be fired. In fact, Mr. Tumey reminded me when we discussed asking for your help that our files are strictly confidential."

"I understand," Nancy said, disappointed.

"No," Joyce said. "Nancy, I'm desperate to get to the truth. At this point, I don't care about bending the rules or even breaking them. If you think it'll work, I say go for it."

"Are you sure? I don't want to jeopardize your job."

"It's already in jeopardy," Joyce said. "Look, there's an end-of-season dinner tomorrow night, a sort of thank-you to the employees. Everyone will be there, and the office will be deserted. I'll let you in then. No one should find out. It'll be fine. Okay?"

"Okay," Nancy agreed. "If you say so. Thanks."

"Thank *you*," Joyce said. "Try to get some sleep, and enjoy your day tomorrow."

Sleep. Not a bad idea, Nancy thought. Her eyes hurt, her feet hurt, her brain hurt. As soon as she returned from dinner, she changed into her pajamas and crawled under the cool, white sheets.

The next thing she knew, George was showering after her morning jog. Even Bess was awake and munching a chocolate croissant.

"I checked on the Sleuths. They're all sleeping. They're exhausted," Bess informed Nancy. "Just like us."

George toweled off her hair as she emerged from the bathroom. "What's on the agenda for today?"

"Andrea might get out of the hospital," Bess said. "The van might get fixed. We might go home."

"*I'm* not going home," Nancy said. "I've got big plans tonight. But I hope you can."

Bess looked at the clock. "I guess it's still too early to call the garage."

Nancy nodded. "I think," she said, "I'm going back to the computer lab. Do you know how they have all those family trees online? Maybe I can figure out whether Andrea really is related to the Castle family."

There was a knock on the door.

Bess rolled her eyes. "Here we go again. At your service," she called as she flung open the door.

"Andrea!" she exclaimed.

"May I come in?"

Nancy could see that Andrea's face was drawn and pale.

"Of course." Bess moved aside to let her pass. "Please. Sit down. How are you? How did you get here?"

"I took a taxi," Andrea replied. "And I'm feeling better. Or at least I was, until I heard what you were saying just now."

Bess looked perplexed. "What?"

"About me. Why are you checking up on me behind my back? If you have a question, I wish you'd ask me to my face."

"I'm sorry, Andrea," Nancy said. "We've developed some pressing questions in the last day, and you haven't been available to answer them. Frankly, we had reason to doubt that you'd answer them truthfully."

Andrea leaned back against the pillow. "I'm sorry you've come to that conclusion. May I ask why?"

Nancy explained what had happened in her meeting with Mr. Castle the day before. She told Andrea about the lab finding rubber cement on Bess's wrapper, the realization that Andrea had apparently lied about where she bought the chocolates and finally the tombstone Kenny had found in the haunted house that led

Nancy to think Andrea might be related to the Castles.

"You're right," Andrea said simply.

"I'm right?" Nancy repeated.

"I'm related to the Castles. If you can call it a relationship."

"I don't understand, Andrea," Bess said. "Why didn't you tell us?"

"I didn't think it was any of your business. I didn't want anyone to know. It was a mistake." Andrea's voice was low. "I'm sorry."

"All right." Bess reached out and took her hand. "But tell us now. Please tell us what's going on."

"Okay." Andrea nodded. "Remember hearing the story of poor Robert Castle, the immigrant who founded Royal Chocolates? Well, Joyce left out some important information. His real name was Roberto Cassella, and he didn't start Royal Chocolates by himself. The whole thing was his brother's idea. Sal Cassella. My grandfather. But then they had some sort of disagreement. My great-uncle disowned his brother and changed his name. Somehow, he wound up with the company, all the money, everything."

"Wow," Bess said. "That's terrible."

"I'm not surprised about that tombstone Kenny found. It was probably an inside joke. Robert Castle, Senior, was determined to bury his identity as a Cassella. He didn't want any of us getting our hands on his money. Ever."

"But aren't you entitled to it?" Bess asked. "I mean, if your grandfather helped found the company . . ."

Andrea shook her head. "I'm related to the Castles by blood, but that's all. Robert Castle arranged things legally so that the Cassellas wouldn't have any claims on Royal Chocolates. By law, it's as though we're not even family."

"That's awful," George said. "Can't you do anything about it?"

Andrea closed her eyes. "I don't care. I really don't care, George. It's been this way all my life. I just wanted the right to apply for an educational grant for the Sleuths, the same way anyone else could apply. But when I tried, they wouldn't let me. They wouldn't even talk to me."

"Why?" Nancy asked. "Why would they be so unfair?"

"I wish I knew," Andrea said. "Poor Joyce—I know she felt sorry for me by the third time I called. She did what she could. She offered a discounted rate for our trip to the park—a consolation, I guess. She even mailed me some chocolate bars." Andrea propped herself up on her elbows. "This is the part you're waiting to hear. One of those bars was the winning one. The grand prize wrapper."

"Oh." Bess reacted as this sank in. "Oh! *My* wrapper."

"I was so shocked when I saw it," Andrea said. "I actually thought maybe it was Joyce's secret way of helping me with the Sleuths' finances. Then I realized that was ridiculous. It would be illegal to tamper with the outcome of the contest. Anyhow, I wasn't even eligible to claim the prize because of my relation to the Castles. Pretty ironic, if you ask me, since they won't have anything to do with me."

"That's when you decided to glue the wrapper back on and give it to Bess," George said.

"That's right," Andrea confirmed. "And I really did buy all the other chocolates at the park that first day we were here. I never thought that would wind up being an issue. I'm not very good at lying. Obviously, I don't have much practice."

"But why didn't you tell us what was going on?" Bess asked.

"I didn't want to get you mixed up in it," Andrea explained. "I was relying on your basic human decency, Bess. I was pretty sure I could count on you to do the right thing and contribute some of the money back to the Sleuths." Andrea looked Bess in the eye. "And you did. It would have worked, if it weren't for one thing: Diana had already claimed the prize."

"This is all starting to make sense now," Nancy

said slowly. "Except if *yours* is the real winning wrapper, where did Diana get hers? And why has she been spying on us since we got here?"

"I have no idea about any of that." Andrea's eyes went from Bess to George to Nancy. "I'm sorry for misleading you. I hope you believe me."

"So you're saying the van accident and the peanut butter accident—they *were* accidents?" George asked.

Before Andrea could respond, there was another knock at the door.

Laura bounced into the room as soon as Bess cracked open the door. "We're on TV!" she announced.

Nancy flipped on the television set, and Laura changed the channel until she found the local morning news. They were running a story about the Royal Chocolates contest.

Diana's picture flashed across the screen.

"Hey," George said a moment later. "There you are, Bess."

Bess's cheeks turned red. "That's a terrible picture. Where did they get that?"

"Where did they get the story, period?" Nancy murmured.

"Shh," Andrea said. She was listening intently.

The program cut to a shot of a reporter standing at the entrance to the Kings Commons parking lot.

"Could you offer an official comment about the Crown Jewels contest controversy, Mr. Tumey?"

There was a close-up of John Tumey, his irritated scowl filling the screen.

"No comment," he growled.

The camera pulled back to show his car pulling away from the gate. Nancy's heart pounded when she saw the shot. Mr. Tumey was driving a mid-size white car.

"Hey," Laura said. "That looks like the car that ran us off the road at Jungle Kingdom!"

12

News Flash

Nancy squinted at the tiny picture on the television screen. "That's a common enough automobile model. But you're right, Laura. It looks like the car that ran us off the road."

Laura finally took her eyes off the TV and noticed her surroundings. "Andrea!" she exclaimed. "You're back. Are you okay?"

"I'm fine," Andrea assured her. "And very glad to be here, too."

Laura grabbed Andrea's hand and pulled her off the bed. "Come on. Come say hi to everybody. They'll all want to see you. We were so worried. Are we going home today?"

Even after Bess closed the door, Nancy

could hear their chatter all the way down the hall.

"I'd sure like to know how I wound up on the news," Bess said. "Hey—you know what? Maybe that person who called Hannah really *was* a reporter, Nan. Maybe she was working on the story we just saw. Do you think that's who was looking us up in the Royal computer lab?"

"I doubt it," George said. "Why would the reporter use the computers here? She must have the Internet at the TV station."

"She obviously came here to work on her story," Bess pointed out. "We just saw her on TV, standing in front of the chocolate factory. Maybe she had some down time while she was here and decided to put it to good use."

"I'm more concerned with where she got the story idea," Nancy said. "We know nobody from Royal talked to the press in an official capacity. They were trying their hardest to keep the wrapper mix-up quiet. Joyce said Diana doesn't even know about the problems with the contest."

"I guess she knows now," George observed. "It's going to be all over the news."

"That's true." Nancy muted the TV with the remote control.

"I don't get it," Bess said. "Who could have leaked the story?"

"Besides the corporate spy," Nancy said, "there's only one other person I know of with a motive to make things rough for Royal."

"Andrea?" George guessed.

"Wait," Bess said. "Andrea wouldn't do something like that."

"I'd like to believe that, Bess," Nancy said. "I sympathize with her situation, and I'm glad she finally came clean with us. But did she tell the whole truth? We can't be sure, can we?"

Bess sighed. "I like Andrea. She's trying to do a good thing."

"I agree," Nancy said. "I like her, too. I just can't forget Mr. Castle's face when he heard me mention Andrea's name. I know he thought she staged her accidents to give Royal a bad rap. And when you combine those accidents with this news leak, I'm sorry. I have to wonder."

"But what about the Pleasant spy?" Bess asked.

Nancy nodded. "I know. It's possible that a high-level Royal employee is the corporate spy. If so, that person would be aware of the problems with the instant-win contest. Maybe he or she decided to leak that information to the press to give Royal a bad name. If too many people lost faith in Royal they would stop buying Royal products, and the business would really suffer. I'm sure that even Royal's instant-win contests would become less effective at attracting new customers. Their stock prices would go down, and Pleasant would find itself a big winner."

"I bet it's that nasty Mr. Tumey," Bess suggested. "I bet he's the spy."

"That thought crossed my mind," Nancy said. "Besides Joyce, he's the only person who knows I'm working on this case. I know we don't have proof that the car that ran us off the road was his. But if it was, maybe he was trying to scare us off the case before we figured out who the spy was."

Bess had begun pacing. "So what are you going to do next, Nan?"

The phone rang.

Nancy held up her hand. "Answer the phone."

The caller was from the auto repair shop. He said the van was fixed and could be picked up whenever they were ready.

"Yes!" Andrea said with feeling when she returned to the room. "We can all go home this afternoon."

"That's great." Nancy replaced the receiver. "But I can't go with you."

"Why not?" Andrea's voice cracked.

"I need to spend another night at the park. There's something I have to take care of before I leave."

Andrea bit her lip. "So you're going to leave us short one chaperon?"

"We'll manage," George said cheerfully. "We've managed so far, right?"

"I guess." Andrea stared at the floor.

Nancy knew Andrea wanted to know what Nancy's plans for tonight were. Nancy just didn't feel comfortable giving away any information about the investigation. She hoped Joyce's files would give her the evidence she needed to identify the spy, and to get to the bottom of the instant-win mystery. More than anything, she hoped they would be able to prove that Andrea was telling them the truth.

"I'll let you pack." Andrea excused herself. "I'm going to take a cab to pick up the van. I guess I'll be paying for it with more money I don't have. I'll see you later."

"Hopefully, she *will* have that money the next time I see her," Nancy said after Andrea had left.

"I'm keeping my fingers crossed," Bess said.

George tossed a pile of clothes in Bess's direction. "If we're going to leave today, you'd better start packing. It might take several hours."

Bess dragged both her suitcases out of the closet. "Let's not forget, I'm the one who brought the blazer. It came in handy, didn't it?"

"I see it's the only thing actually left on a hanger. I guess that's because *Nancy's* the one who took care of it."

"Do you think you could argue quietly?" Nancy teased them. "I need to make a phone call."

While Bess and George packed, Nancy phoned the news station that had aired the instant-win story. She was surprised when the operator connected her directly to the reporter, Deborah Hui.

"Hi," Nancy began. "My name is Nancy Drew, and—"

"And you're involved in the Royal Chocolates instant-win scandal," Deborah said. "I'm doing a follow-up story on the evening news tonight. Do you have some information for me?"

"Not exactly," Nancy said. "In fact, we were hoping to keep this out of the media until the identity of the winner was settled."

"Sorry, but the news is already out there. We have to do our job." She paused. "Wait a minute. You're the one who's some kind of detective, right? Let me guess. You want to know my source on the story."

"I was hoping you might be able to help me, yes," Nancy said.

"I'm sure you realize it would be unethical for me to reveal that information," Deborah replied.

"How ethical is it to air a story without trying to speak with all the people involved? You didn't try to contact my friend Bess Marvin, for example. Whoever your source was—"

"You're not going to find out who she was," Deborah interrupted, "so you might as well stop trying."

110

She, Nancy thought. That was something. If Deborah's source was female, that would eliminate John Tumey.

"Thanks for your time," Nancy said. She hung up before Deborah could make another pitch for Nancy to talk to her on the evening news.

So John Tumey wasn't the person who talked to Deborah, Nancy realized. That didn't mean he wasn't involved. Maybe he was working with Diana or Andrea. Maybe one of them had given Deborah the story.

Nancy thought about Diana's strange behavior since they had arrived. All along, they had assumed Diana didn't know that Bess had come forward with another winning wrapper because Joyce hadn't told her. But what if someone else had told Diana about Bess's wrapper? Nancy wondered. If Diana was working with the corporate spy and the spy knew about the wrapper, *the spy* could have told her. That would explain why Diana had been eavesdropping on them and acting hostile. She was probably desperate to find out whether her chances of winning the grand prize were ruined.

Bess snapped her fingers in front of Nancy's face. "Earth to Nan."

"Sorry," Nancy said. "I was just thinking."

"Are you sure you're okay here by yourself?" Bess asked. "I could stay if you want me to."

"That's sweet, Bess, but I'll be fine. And Andrea definitely needs you," Nancy said.

George grunted as she heaved Bess's suitcase onto the bed. "You need *us*, too, to help you cart this stuff out of here. Maybe one of the Sleuths can give you a science tip to make these bags easier to carry. Like a lever. Or gee—how about packing lighter?"

Nancy held the door open while Bess and George dragged their bags into the hall. "Make sure you call me tonight, so I know you got home safely," she said.

Their good bye was cut short by the ringing phone. "Grand Central Station," Nancy answered.

"Nancy?" Joyce's voice sounded uncertain.

"Hi, Joyce. I'm sorry to answer that way. It's just that it's been hectic around here. What can I do for you?"

"I don't suppose you happened to see the news this morning," Joyce said.

"In fact, I did." Nancy sat on the bed, preparing herself for a long conversation. "Do you have any idea where the press heard about the contest problems?"

"None." Joyce sighed. "But Mr. Castle went through the roof when he saw the story."

"I bet," Nancy said. "I wish I could say I had some leads for you, but I don't. I did stumble across something else today."

Nancy went on to explain about Andrea's release from the hospital and her story that Joyce had sent her the instant-win wrapper after Andrea's futile attempts to contact Robert Castle.

"I don't want to sound as though I'm questioning Andrea's account of what happened," Nancy said. "But I was hoping you could just verify for me that you did mail Andrea those chocolates."

"Gosh." Joyce sounded strained. "You can't believe how many promotional materials I send out every day. It's quite possible Andrea was on my list. I wish I could say for sure, but there's no way I can remember."

"You don't have any records? Nothing?"

"Sorry," Joyce said. "If we kept files on freebies, we wouldn't have room for anything else."

Nancy drummed her fingers on the nightstand. She had hoped Joyce would be able to give her an easy answer. "Wait a minute," she said. "Andrea didn't mention to you that she's related to Robert Castle?"

"Related to . . . ?" Joyce trailed off. "Her last name is Cassella. Of course. I can't believe I didn't realize that myself."

Joyce's reaction surprised Nancy. She had been under the impression from Andrea that Joyce was aware of their relationship.

"No wonder Mr. Castle was so upset after he met with you," Joyce went on. "He's incredibly

113

suspicious of his estranged family members. He always thinks they're dreaming up new schemes to get to his money. Not that I think that's what Andrea's doing," Joyce added hastily.

"You've been very understanding about all this," Nancy said.

"The Golden Rule," Joyce said. "Just because my bosses walk all over me doesn't mean I like to walk all over other people."

"Joyce, do any of your bosses besides Mr. Tumey know that I'm working with you on this investigation?" Nancy asked.

"Absolutely not," Joyce said. "Unless—"

"Unless?"

"I can't vouch for what Mr. Tumey does, of course. If he told someone, I wouldn't know about it. He's not fond of filling me in on lots of things."

She doesn't trust John Tumey, Nancy thought to herself. Was Joyce trying to find a tactful way of telling Nancy she thought Mr. Tumey had been giving out information too freely?

"You didn't tell Mr. Tumey I'd be going through the files tonight," Nancy said.

"Are you kidding?" Joyce laughed nervously. "He'd have me fired. But he'll never know. It turns out he's off-site all afternoon at a meeting with a client. He probably won't even come back for the dinner. It starts at five-thirty, by the way.

Why don't you come over at six. I'll buzz you up, then I'll slip out to go to the dinner. Does that work for you?"

"It sounds great," Nancy said. She thanked Joyce for her help.

Now, she wondered, what was she going to do until six o'clock?

It was Wednesday, she thought. If she went back to the computer lab, Patsy should be there. Maybe Patsy would remember the person who was searching online for information about the Sleuths.

The lab was busy. Nancy had to wait almost half an hour before Patsy was available to speak with her. In the meantime, she heard Patsy explain to two frantic students how to retrieve their lost data.

Nancy thought Patsy seemed both competent and friendly. But Patsy's smile faded when she heard Nancy's question.

"Users at this terminal two days ago? Um . . . isn't there anything else I could help you with? A computer question, maybe?"

"I know it's a strange request," Nancy said. "And a long shot. I just hoped that maybe the person asked you a question or made an impression somehow."

"Wait a second! I do remember something," Patsy said suddenly. "This lady definitely stood out. She *was* sitting at this terminal. It was toward the end of the day. And I had to tell her, like, three times to quit eating chocolate in the lab."

Nancy asked Patsy to describe the woman. Not only did the description fit Diana, but Patsy also mentioned the woman's silent husband, who sat in a chair beside her the whole time.

Nancy thanked Patsy. "I'll let you get back to work," she said as a user waved his hand frantically for Patsy's help.

Nancy decided to take a walk through the English garden to clear her head.

So it seemed Diana was the woman who had been doing research on Nancy and the Sleuths. Now what?

If Diana really was the woman in the computer lab, *why* was she searching for information? How did she even know their names? Somebody must have told her, Nancy realized. But who? The corporate spy? Or John Tumey? *Was* John Tumey the corporate spy?

After wandering around the park, Nancy took the elevator to the top of the Royal Observatory. From there she had a breathtaking view of the green fields surrounding the park and the shimmering pool at Water Wonderland.

It was surprising, she thought, to see how many people were moving around on the grounds. Workers walked in and out of the chocolate factory. Waves of newcomers continued to pour in through the main gate.

Nancy's gaze stopped at the administration building, which seemed an oasis of calm in the middle of chaos. There was a courtyard behind the offices, and there a man and woman stood alone, talking. Nancy squinted at the woman's yellow-flowered hat, and the man's familiar bald head. "John Tumey and Diana!" she whispered.

Nancy remembered Joyce telling her that Mr. Tumey was away this afternoon to meet with a client. So why was he here, and with Diana? What was going on?

13

Thrown for a Loop

Had Mr. Tumey lied to Joyce about his plans this afternoon? Nancy asked herself. He said he was meeting with a client. Surely Diana wasn't a client.

Nancy realized that there could be a perfectly good reason for Mr. Tumey to meet with Diana. They could be discussing the contest. But why would Joyce think Mr. Tumey was somewhere else? And why were they meeting in an isolated area behind the building instead of in Mr. Tumey's office?

As Nancy expected, by the time she got back to the ground and made her way to the administration building, Diana and John Tumey had both disappeared. There was no chance of eavesdropping on their conversation.

Nancy checked her watch. In another couple of hours she could meet Joyce. She couldn't wait to search John Tumey's office and maybe find some answers.

After a leisurely early dinner, Nancy returned to the administration building and dialed the number for Joyce's office. A moment later she was buzzed inside.

Joyce seemed harried when Nancy arrived on the fifth floor. "I've got to get to this dinner pronto," she explained to Nancy. "Mr. Castle was very anxious that I be there." She hurriedly demonstrated where Nancy might find various files in the suite of offices.

"Feel free to go through my office. Mr. Tumey's, too. I'm sorry, but I wasn't able to get a key to Mr. Castle's."

"That's okay. I think the chance that he's the corporate spy is pretty close to zero."

"I hate to ask you this, but I'll also need you to turn off the lights." Joyce reached out and flipped the switch. "We used to have round-the-clock security until our budget cutbacks. Now, with the new alarm system, the guards go off-duty at eleven. In the meantime, I don't want them to suspect someone's snooping up here." Joyce handed her a huge flashlight.

"Thanks," Nancy said. "This'll work a lot better than my penlight."

"Okay," Joyce said. "I'll be back in a couple of hours. Good luck." She hurried to the elevator, leaving Nancy to decide which of the dozens of file drawers to open first.

Nancy turned toward Mr. Tumey's office. She should probably start there, she decided. Her heart sank when she saw the long row of file cabinets lining the area behind his desk and behind the door, not to mention the stacks of folders on top of his credenza.

Mr. Tumey's computer screen glowed invitingly in the darkness. If I had classified information, Nancy thought, I'd keep it hidden on a hard drive rather than printed out and in a file.

She sat down at Mr. Tumey's computer, pleased that she didn't need a password to access his files. On the desktop, she saw an icon for an electronic address book. This would be a good place to start looking for information, Nancy decided.

With little trouble, Nancy found listings for both Diana and Pleasant Candies. This was not unexpected. In fact, Mr. Tumey probably had good reason to contact both Diana and Pleasant Candies.

Nancy decided it might be worthwhile to dial the Pleasant number to see who answered.

The phone was answered on the first ring by a

woman with a low, soothing voice. "Maggie Fitzwilliam."

Nancy was so astonished that she nearly dropped the phone. Maggie Fitzwilliam was the president and CEO of Pleasant Candies!

Nancy hung up hastily. She wondered whether Maggie Fitzwilliam had caller ID and could trace her call. Had she just tipped off Pleasant that she was checking up on them? she worried.

There was no way, Nancy thought, that Mr. Tumey would be doing normal Royal Chocolates business with Maggie Fitzwilliam on her personal phone line. Nancy had to assume it was her personal line, since she had answered it after hours.

John Tumey must be the corporate spy, Nancy decided. As she clicked the mouse to close the entry in his address book, she noticed something startling. This entry had been added to John's file today. On a hunch, she checked Diana's address—it was also dated today.

If John were the spy, Nancy knew he would have been using these numbers for months. That didn't make sense at all. These numbers had just been added to the address book today. *Had* Mr. Tumey really been using them? Or was someone just trying to make it *seem* that he had been? Did someone want to make him appear guilty when Nancy accessed his computer?

No one knew Nancy was going to his office but

Joyce. Was Joyce trying to set John up? Nancy asked herself. Why would she do that unless *she* was the corporate spy?

Nancy remembered Joyce saying she'd rather work with Nancy than against her. Maybe she'd asked for Nancy's help because of Nancy's determination to investigate. Maybe she had thought she could control the direction of Nancy's investigation and steer the blame away from herself—and onto John Tumey.

Nancy hurried into Joyce's office, knowing that Joyce would expect her to search there. Joyce would have been careful to get rid of any evidence that might make her look guilty.

Nancy imagined Joyce making preparations for Nancy to snoop in her office. Any computer files that might provide useful information would have been deleted. Any incriminating papers would have been taken home or shredded.

Nancy had a sudden memory of the information she had heard Patsy giving the students in the computer lab about retrieving lost files. When files were deleted from the hard drive of the computer, they weren't actually gone. They were sent temporarily to a place called the Recycle Bin. After a few days the computer would automatically purge the information in the Recycle Bin. But until then, those files should still be there—and easily accessible.

Nancy found the Recycle Bin icon and double clicked on it.

Sure enough, she found a list of files Joyce had deleted that morning.

Nancy opened the first file. It was a letter addressed to Andrea, care of the Science Sleuths.

Nancy could hardly believe her good fortune. This was obviously information Joyce thought was hidden forever from prying eyes.

"Dear Ms. Cassella," she read. "Thank you for your interest in applying for an educational grant from Royal Chocolates. It is with regret that I must inform you Mr. Castle has declined to grant you an interview.

"However, we are pleased to provide you with discounted tickets to Kings Commons so that you may share the Royal Chocolates experience with your students. We also hope that you will enjoy the candy bars I have enclosed. Please note that these do not contain nuts, so there is no need for concern regarding your food allergy.

"We look forward to seeing you at Kings Commons. Please stop in the office and say hello when you visit.

"Sincerely, Joyce Palmer."

Nancy printed out this letter and tucked it into her purse. She moved on to the next file, which was a similar letter to Diana. This one thanked Diana for her interest in producing marketing materials for Royal Chocolates. Joyce added that she hoped Diana and Phil continued to be loyal consumers of Royal Chocolates, and she was enclosing several chocolate bars for their enjoyment.

Wow, Nancy thought. Joyce must have sent a winning wrapper to Andrea, and another one to Diana. She was the one who ruined Royal's contest. Nancy couldn't believe she hadn't realized it before. Who better to pull all the strings than the person in charge of the contest?

Furthermore, Joyce knew about Andrea's peanut allergy. She must have been behind the Kings Cup mix-up. Earlier that day, Joyce had told Nancy that she didn't remember talking with Andrea and had no records of such transactions on file. She must have been lying. And this letter proved that Andrea was telling the truth. Besides giving Bess the winning wrapper, she'd done nothing to deceive anyone.

Nancy sent this file to the fancy color printer and heard a high-pitched *ding*. For a moment she thought it was the computer. Then she realized it was the elevator. The elevator was coming to the fifth floor. Nobody was supposed to be there. Was it Joyce? Was she coming back already?

Nancy turned off the flashlight and ducked behind Joyce's desk.

Soon she heard whispered voices. "I can't believe we're actually breaking into the corporate offices," said one.

"What else were we supposed to do? No one's going to help us. We have to help ourselves."

"I think all this chocolate has made us behave in ways we never would have dreamed possible."

"Give me a break. It's not the chocolate. It's the million dollars."

Diana and Phil, Nancy thought. They must be trying to get to the bottom of the mystery, too. Just as she'd been convinced that Diana had forged the winning wrapper, Diana must think Bess had, Nancy realized.

"That money's ours, and we're obviously not going to get it unless we do something drastic. Not only did Bess Marvin and her friends cheat, they went and got Joyce on their side."

"You don't know that for sure, Di."

"When I met with John Tumey today, he practically admitted it," Diana replied.

So *that's* what she and Mr. Tumey had talked about, Nancy thought.

"It makes me so mad," Diana continued. "I thought Mr. Tumey would be impartial, and that he would understand why I wanted in on the investigation. But he just kept saying the matter would be handled internally. I definitely got the impression he doesn't like Joyce, though. I think she's on her way out."

Nancy tried to make herself smaller as Diana and Phil passed by the door to Joyce's office. She breathed a sigh of relief as they walked by without stopping.

"At least one good thing came from your meeting with John," Phil pointed out. "You watched him punch in the building access code, so we could let ourselves in." He sighed. "I just wish there were some other way."

"We don't have time to waste," Diana said. "We're going home tomorrow. The Royal people aren't trying to get to the truth. That means we've got to do it ourselves. Otherwise, we might never get that prize. Even worse, they might make us look like criminals. What if they try to say *we* forged the wrapper? Have you thought about that, Phil? I mean, our business is publishing. Royal turned down our proposal to do work for them, so we should hate them, right? We couldn't look much guiltier."

"They could never prove it," Phil said. "We didn't do anything wrong."

"I bet they could find a way. At the very least, they could tie up our money for a very long time. It's our money, Phil."

Nancy strained to hear Phil's reply as they moved farther down the hall. Then she heard a door close. They must be looking in the cabinets behind Mr. Tumey's door, Nancy thought. Now was her chance to sneak out. She didn't want to risk being caught. She stood and stretched gingerly. Then there was a creaking noise behind her. Before she could turn around, a heavy object was smashed over her head. Everything went black.

When Nancy awoke, she had no idea how much time had passed. Her hand went to an egg-size lump on her head. The big flashlight lay beside her, and the door to the supply closet was open, with Crown Jewels tote bags spilled onto the floor.

"Get up," Joyce ordered in a fierce whisper. "Let's go."

Slowly Nancy held on to the desk and pulled herself upright. Joyce was holding a pointed object against her back. In the darkness Nancy couldn't tell for sure whether it was a knife. But her head was throbbing so hard she knew she could never get away. She couldn't outrun Joyce; she didn't think she could run at all.

Joyce led her down the back stairs and into the parking lot. Nancy shivered. The moon was a slender crescent, and the stars were dim. The world seemed cold and dark and silent. The dinner must be over, Nancy thought. The park was closed—the factory deserted.

Joyce shoved Nancy into her car. A white, mid-size car identical to John Tumey's.

"Company car," she explained.

Nancy closed her eyes. "Where are you taking me?" she asked.

"You'll see," Joyce said.

Nancy's head felt as though it were floating above the rest of her. She could hear her heart pounding in her ears. She fought the fuzzy feeling, fought to stay awake, but she could not.

When she came to again, she felt something moving beneath her. It wasn't an automobile this time. She felt the wind in her hair. She opened her eyes and saw blackness. Then she felt herself plunging down into darkness, and her stomach moved into her throat. She was on Royal Pain. She didn't know how, but she was on Royal Pain, alone and in the dark. The car was pitching ahead, carrying all its momentum forward as it thundered into the first loop. Nancy felt instinctively for the restraint across her chest. There was none. She was unprotected against the force that would rip her from the car the moment it turned upside down. In that split second she realized she was about to be flung from the car onto the ground so far below she could not even see it.

14

Recipe for Danger

Nancy jerked her hands over her head and pulled the restraint down and across her chest just as she felt the world turning upside down. Her entire weight caught against the bar and then she was whipped backward against the seat.

Now the hills and loops passed in a blur as Nancy's mind raced along with the ride.

Would the car stop by itself? What if it didn't? What if she rode again and again, in an endless cycle?

Then Nancy felt the brakes pull, and the car stopped abruptly. She took a deep breath as she squinted into the darkness. The ride had halted several feet from the gate. Her knees trembling, she stepped out of the car. Slowly, clutching the cars for support, she crawled along the track until she reached the solid wood platform.

She stood for a moment, peering out over the darkened park and listening to the night sounds of Jungle Kingdom animals and cars on the distant highway.

Was Joyce still out there? Nancy asked herself. She didn't know, but she definitely wasn't going to wait to find out.

There was no new sound or movement as she climbed down the steps and slipped unnoticed into the night.

Nancy knew there were no guards, no friendly park workers to run to. There were phones, though, and she had to get to a phone.

In the distance, something at the chocolate factory caught Nancy's eye. She thought she saw a beam of light in a second-story window. Almost instantly, it disappeared. Had she imagined it? Nancy wondered. But then she glimpsed it again. Now it was in the next room, its reflection bouncing and flickering off the glass. Someone must be walking through the building. Probably with a flashlight, she thought.

Nancy squinted at her watch. It was midnight. No one should be in the factory at this hour. What was going on?

Then Nancy spotted two shadowy figures running toward the building. Even in the distance, Nancy recognized the loping stride of George and the small, hurried footsteps of Bess. What were they doing here? she thought. She hoped they wouldn't go into the building. What if Joyce was in there? Nancy touched the spot where Joyce had smashed the flashlight into her head. What if Bess and George were about to find themselves face to face with the woman who had just tried to kill her?

Nancy's breath came in gasps by the time she reached the pay phone. Her head was pounding. She had no money, and her purse was somewhere in Joyce's office. Her emergency change must have fallen out of her pockets on that horrible ride. Nancy knew there was only one thing to do. She picked up the receiver and dialed 911.

"I need police assistance at the Royal Chocolates factory," Nancy managed to say. "I was just assaulted."

"Stay on the line, please," the operator instructed. "I need you to tell me exactly what happened."

"No time." Nancy struggled to catch her breath. "Lives may be in danger. Please hurry."

She left the receiver dangling in her haste to get to the factory. She had to stop Bess and George before they found Joyce.

By the time she reached the factory entrance,

Bess and George were nowhere in sight. Through the door, Nancy heard the whir of conveyor belts. She smelled freshly melted chocolate. The security keypad was lit up, and the door had been left ajar.

What was going on? Nancy wondered. Who had unlocked the door? Who had started up the machinery in the middle of the night? Was somebody trying to lure her inside?

Nancy was inclined to ignore her natural curiosity and stay outdoors until the police arrived, but she was worried about Bess and George. If they had gone inside, she had to find them.

She pulled open the door and slipped inside.

There was a scream and a purse came crashing down on Nancy's head.

"Nan!" Bess shrieked. "I thought you were a criminal. I'm sorry."

Nancy put a hand up to her aching head. "It's okay. It's just me."

"George and I thought you were in here. We thought you were in trouble," Bess said. "I'm so glad you're all right."

"She's not all right," George said. "Can't you tell she's in pain? When have you ever known Nancy to moan?"

"*I'm* not moaning." Nancy shushed Bess as she opened her mouth to say something. She listened intently. "I do hear it, George. Someone needs help."

"Help!" A female voice echoed weakly in the enormous, empty room. Then came a long, soft whimper.

"Wait." Nancy stopped Bess and George. "I called the police. The safe thing to do is to go outside and wait for them to come."

"Yeah, right," Bess said. "Like you're going to leave someone in trouble."

"It's coming from over there." George strode toward the cooling tunnels.

Nancy put a hand on George's shoulder as she felt along the wall for the lights. "Be careful."

"Okay," George said. "Nan, what's going on here?"

"It's a long story," Nancy answered. "But I don't know what happened to Phil or Diana. The last time I saw them, they were in danger without realizing it. I'm afraid they may be hurt."

"What about you?" Bess asked. "We were so afraid something happened to you."

"How did you know?" Nancy said. "What made you decide to come back to Kings Commons?"

"We said we'd call you when we got home, remember?" Bess steadied herself as her feet found an uneven patch of floor. "When you weren't back in your motel room by nine, I started to get very nervous. That's when I called George. I was sure she would tell me I was being paranoid, but she was just as worried as I was. Within ten minutes,

133

she was at my house. We got here in record time. It was the scariest ride of my life."

Nancy chuckled. "Don't talk to me about scary rides. You wouldn't believe the one Joyce just treated me to."

"Joyce?" Bess gasped. "Oh, Nan—are you saying Joyce is behind all this crazy stuff? Joyce is the corporate spy?"

Nancy nodded. "At any rate, she just tried to kill me by sticking me on Royal Pain without a restraint when I was unconscious."

"Unconscious?" Bess tried to look into Nancy's face in the dim light. "Nan, are you okay?"

"I think so," Nancy murmured. "I wish I could find this light switch."

"I'm sorry we didn't get to you sooner," George said. "When we pulled into the parking lot, we saw that there was somebody in the chocolate factory. We knew something must be wrong. And we were afraid something bad had happened to you. We never thought to look for you in the amusement park."

"It's okay. I can't believe you came at all. Anyhow," Nancy said brightly, "all's well that ends well. I think."

"That's where you're wrong," said a voice from the corner of the room. Joyce's voice.

The moaning stopped when Joyce began to speak. It was Joyce all along. She was trying to lure them inside and trap them, Nancy thought. She'd wanted them to come inside the factory. What was she going to do to them now?

"The police are on their way," Nancy told Joyce. "If you try to hurt George and Bess, you're only going to find yourself in more trouble."

"Do you know what the police are going to find when they get here?" Joyce asked. "A wonderful treat. A new flavor of Royal candy. Chocolate Nancy."

Joyce reached out and flipped a switch. Nancy heard the grinding of machinery overhead. She looked up to see a huge vat moving forward. Thinking back to the chocolate factory tour, Nancy remembered that that vat would be filled with melted chocolate heated to 150°F. Now it was being tipped forward, and a stream of churning, boiling chocolate came pouring down, straight toward their heads.

15

Wrapping Up

Nancy saw that Bess was rooted in place, unable even to scream. Nancy shoved her into motion and out of the path of the molten chocolate. As she and George dove for cover, Nancy felt a few scalding drops brush against her face as wave after wave of burning liquid plopped harmlessly onto the floor.

Next came the sound of running as Joyce tried to get away. Before Nancy realized what was happening, George leaped through the air and wrestled Joyce to the ground with a flying tackle.

"Ow!" Joyce cried. She was facedown in the chocolate, cooler now as it spread thinly all over the floor.

"I hate chocolate!" Joyce spat a mouthful in George's direction. "I didn't know you were bringing reinforcements, Nancy."

Nancy had groped her way over to the packaging area of the factory. Here, at last, she found the light switch.

Joyce hid her face as the brightness blinded her.

Nancy quickly sifted through wrappers and boxes until she found packing tape, which she threw across the room to Bess.

"Someone at Pleasant must have paid you a lot of money to make trouble for Royal. Was it worth it?" Nancy asked Joyce as George and Bess wrapped several feet of tape around her wrists and ankles.

"Of course not." Joyce squirmed in the chocolate puddle. "I never thought this would happen."

"A little money is one thing," Nancy agreed. "Did you ever think you would try to kill someone?"

"Look," Joyce said. "I didn't mean for it to happen that way. You have to understand, I was desperate."

George ripped the tape with her teeth. "Original, too."

"Not really. I needed an instant plan when I heard you come in. I thought Nancy was dead already. How else would you kill someone in a chocolate factory—boiling you in a vat of choco-late was all I could do."

Bess shivered. "I'm glad it didn't work."

"It's not as though I planned to kill anybody," Joyce said. "I didn't think you'd ever figure out I was the spy. I worked my way up through the ranks here at Royal, and put everything I had into this company. You see all the respect and appreci-ation it's gotten me. Nothing but torment from Mr. Tumey every single day.

"Even when I was in high school, I worked here summers in the most boring jobs—box-ing chocolate bars and pushing a button to start Labyrinth. Over and over and over. It wasn't until tonight that I realized what a useful skill that could be. A roller coaster accident. Who would ever suspect me? No one saw me drive you through the gate and put you on that coast-er."

"What about Diana and Phil?" Nancy asked. "What did you do with them?"

"Please," Joyce scoffed. "Given the same infor-mation you had—the same files and documents and computers—they found out nothing. Then they had a little argument about how to spend the instant-win money, and I believe they went home to bed."

"Where were *we* while you were observing them?" Nancy asked.

"In the supply closet," Joyce said. "It was a little tight. Good thing you're thin."

"When you told me you were leaving for the company dinner," Nancy said, "you must have gone back into your office instead. You were hiding in the closet the whole time."

"Bingo," Joyce said. "I thought I had everything covered. If you got off that ride alive, I knew you'd be nosy enough to come back here to see why the factory was churning out chocolate at midnight. You and your friends are bleeding heart types, aren't you, Nancy? And of course you responded to the pitiful cries of a person in need. A little luck, and it all would have worked. I never did have any luck," she complained.

"You want to talk about luck?" Bess said. "I never thought winning a million dollars could feel so unlucky. I'm sure Diana would agree with me."

"You set up Diana and Andrea, didn't you?" Nancy said to Joyce. "You picked people who had ties to Royal who would make believable wrapper forgers. Then you sent them each a winning wrapper."

"I wouldn't call it setting them up," Joyce said. "I provided them with the means to win a million dollars apiece. You can't tell me that did them any harm."

"I thought only one winning wrapper was printed," Bess said. "How did you make two?"

"The same way anyone else would," Joyce said. "I have a nice color printer. I had the instant win code. I forged them." She cleared her throat. "Actually, there's a *third* winning wrapper out there somewhere. The real one. And probably no one will ever claim that prize. Somebody ate that candy and threw away the wrapper. Or maybe it's still sitting on a shelf somewhere. It happens all the time. Instant-win contests are a big joke. But this time, I had to make sure people actually came forward to claim the prize. That's why I targeted Andrea and Diana specifically."

"Which is why you were so shocked when Bess came forward with the winning wrapper," Nancy said. "You were expecting Andrea."

"Your knee is in my back," Joyce spat at George.

"Sorry." George shifted to make Joyce more comfortable.

"Yes, I was expecting Andrea," Joyce told Nancy. "It wasn't until I realized your connection to Andrea that I understood what must have happened. That she must have given the wrapper to Bess, and that Bess obviously had no clue as to what was going on."

"That's when you tried to turn us against Andrea," Bess said. "You tried to make us think she was lying."

"I bet," Nancy added, "you never even told Mr.

Castle that Andrea wanted to speak with him so she could apply for an educational grant."

"That's true," Joyce admitted. "But it wouldn't have changed anything. Mr. Castle wasn't going to talk to her. Trust me. I felt sorry for Andrea. Really, I did. I know how badly Mr. Castle can treat people. So I figured this would work to everyone's advantage. Andrea would get the money for her precious Science Sleuths. And I would get money from Pleasant for making waves at Royal. They even promised that when I couldn't stand it anymore, they'd hire me away from Royal. I was doing an excellent job at this spying business, if I do say so myself. Our profits were decreasing. Pleasant's were increasing."

"Wait a minute." Bess stopped Joyce. "How did you think Andrea was going to collect the instant-win money?"

"That's easy," Andrea said. "Nobody could have proven those wrappers weren't legit—that either Diana or Andrea was a forger. To keep things quiet, Royal would have paid up. It would have worked out great for everybody."

"But Andrea wasn't eligible to claim the prize," Nancy said. "You had to know that."

"No," Joyce replied. "Mr. Castle disinherited her entire side of the family. Legally speaking, that made her perfectly eligible. She just didn't realize it, I guess. The wording is a little confusing in that area."

"Wow," Bess said. "Poor Andrea. All that worry for nothing."

"All your contest fixing would been for nothing," Nancy told Joyce, "if the media didn't find out about Royal's problems. You wanted to make Royal seem untrustworthy in the eyes of the public, so you leaked the contest story to the press."

"You also ran us off the road that day," Bess accused. "And you gave Andrea that horrible allergic reaction."

"It wasn't a big deal," Joyce said. "I just wanted to make Royal look bad and make you suspicious of Andrea. Maybe scare you into taking the kids away from the park before anything bad could happen to them. I figured Nancy would be less of a pain if she wasn't right here, breathing down my neck. But then the van got damaged, and my plan kind of backfired. Things just sort of escalated from there. I never meant for anybody to get hurt."

"Until tonight, you mean." Nancy heard the sound of sirens approaching. "I'm sure the police will be anxious to hear how noble your motives were."

Joyce groaned when she saw Mr. Castle enter with four police officers. "The one bright spot in all this was that I'd hoped never to see you again," she told her boss.

Mr. Castle took in the scene of Joyce, struggling

and spitting and covered in chocolate. "Joyce, I think the feeling is definitely mutual."

Two officers escorted Joyce to the squad car as the other pair took statements from Nancy, Bess, and George.

"I don't know how to thank you," Mr. Castle kept saying. "I can't believe I was so wrong."

When the police had collected all the information they needed, Mr. Castle asked whether there was anything he could do for Nancy and her friends. "At least let me put you up in a nice hotel tonight."

"Tonight?" Nancy laughed. "The sun's coming up as we speak."

"I think we all just want to go home," George said.

"We're really anxious to tell Andrea what happened," Bess added.

"What's going to happen with the contest?" Nancy asked Mr. Castle.

"I'll have to check with the legal department, but I'm fairly certain that the rules state the results must be declared null and void in the event of tampering. Of course, you will receive a substantial reward for your efforts."

Nancy shook her head. "That's not necessary, Mr. Castle. If you want to show your appreciation, maybe you might reconsider the Science Sleuths' application for an educational grant."

"You don't have to ask, Nancy." Mr. Castle flushed slightly. "I read the literature you left me about Andrea's Science Sleuths. I was already feeling ashamed for the way I treated you yesterday. It's obviously an excellent program. The Sleuths are thoroughly deserving of whatever money I can give them."

Nancy looked into his eyes. "I wish *you'd* tell Andrea that, Mr. Castle."

"If she would consent to speak with me, I would be happy to. I look forward to hearing more about the incredible work my cousin is doing. But—" Mr. Castle said.

Bess frowned. "But?"

"You must let me do something for you, too," Mr. Castle insisted. "Wait! I know! Rumor has it you're quite the chocolate fan," he told Bess. "How about a lifetime supply of Crown Jewels bars?"

Bess made a face. "No offense, Mr. Castle. But after what happened tonight, I don't think I want another morsel of chocolate as long as I live."

"Excuse me?" Nancy shook her head. "I'm so tired, I think I must be imagining things. I thought I just heard you say you didn't want to eat any more chocolate."

"My no-chocolate resolution didn't last even a day," Bess lamented the next afternoon as she took a Royal Scepter bar from Kenny.

"We're melting them to see how much is chocolate and how much is almonds," Kenny explained. "Then we're comparing the Pleasant Bar to see which is nuttier."

"I certainly hope the Scepter wins. Our lab says it's twenty-two percent nuttier." Mr. Castle stepped inside the classroom through the back door. Bess exchanged a look with Nancy and George. She showed them that her fingers were crossed.

"Mr. C-Castle," Andrea stammered.

Mr. Castle held up his hand. "Before you throw me out, I hope you'll *hear* me out." He addressed the Sleuths. "How would you like to come back to Kings Commons next year?"

There was a deafening cheer from the children.

"I want you to know that you'll always be welcome in the Kings Commons family. And to make sure you can keep coming back to see us, I have a little present for Andrea." He handed Andrea an envelope.

"I was going to invite you to the park to award you this educational grant," he told Andrea. "But Nancy suggested that I come to River Heights and see the Sleuths in action. I admit, I was motivated as much by guilt as anything else in deciding to give you this money. That's no longer the case. I've been standing here observing you, and it's obvious these children love what they're doing. You have a true gift—all of you. I can only hope you'll forgive me for misjudging you so badly."

"I know you had a busy schedule this week, Mr. Castle. It means a lot to me that you made time for us." Andrea gestured toward the Sleuths. "As they say in physics, for every reaction there is an—"

"Equal and opposite reaction," the Sleuths sang out.

"Very good!" Andrea gingerly took the envelope from Mr. Castle's fingers. "If you can take such a big step, Mr. Castle—"

"Robert," he corrected.

"Robert." Andrea smiled. "If you can take such a big step, I can reach out, too. Thank you."

"Thank you, thank you." The Sleuths clustered around Mr. Castle, showing him their projects and filling the room with laughter.

"We've had a little too much sugar," Andrea apologized.

"It's no different from a typical day at Royal Chocolates," Mr. Castle said.

"Mr. Castle," Kenny said, "we just did a taste test, and Crown Jewels beat Golden Bars two to one. I thought you might like to know that."

"Then I guess you're going to love the box of Crown Jewels bars I brought for the class," Mr. Castle said.

There was a mad rush for the box of chocolate.

As the candy quickly exchanged hands, Andrea came over to Nancy.

"I didn't get a chance to properly thank you, Nancy. Bess and George, too." She smiled as she watched Mr. Castle handing out candy to the children. "None of this would have happened without you. I only wish I'd trusted you with the whole truth from the beginning."

"It doesn't matter." Kenny took a huge bite of his chocolate bar. "They had the Sleuths to help them out."

"Yes," Laura said, "but Nancy's the one who taught us to be Sleuths." She grinned at Nancy. "And she's still the best Sleuth of all."